P9-AGV-145

Among the Hidden

MARGARET PETERSON HADDIX

ALADDIN PAPERBACKS

For John and Janet

First Aladdin Paperbacks edition March 2000

Text copyright ©1998 by Margaret Peterson Haddix
Illustration copyright ©1998 by Cliff Nielsen

Aladdin Paperbacks
An imprint of Simon & Schuster
Children's Publishing Division
1230 Avenue of the Americas
New York, NY 10020

Also available in a Simon & Schuster Books for Young Readers edition.
Designed by Heather Wood
The text for this book was set in Elysium.
Printed and bound in the United States of America

44 43 42 41 40 39 38 37 36

The Library of Congress has cataloged the hardcover edition as follows:
Haddix, Margaret Peterson.
Among the hidden / Margaret Peterson Haddix
p.   cm.
Summary: In a future where the Population Police enforce the law limiting a family to only two children, Luke has lived all his twelve years in isolation and fear on his family's farm, until another "third" convinces him that the government is wrong.
ISBN 0-689-81700-2 (hc.)
[1. Science fiction.] I. Title.   PZ7.H1164Am   1998
[Fic]-dc21   97-33052
0-689-82475-0 (pbk.)

CHAPTER **ONE**

He saw the first tree shudder and fall, far off in the distance. Then he heard his mother call out the kitchen window: "Luke! Inside. Now."

He had never disobeyed the order to hide. Even as a toddler, barely able to walk in the backyard's tall grass, he had somehow understood the fear in his mother's voice. But on this day, the day they began taking the woods away, he hesitated. He took one extra breath of the fresh air, scented with clover and honeysuckle and—coming from far away—pine smoke. He laid his hoe down gently, and savored one last moment of feeling warm soil beneath his bare feet. He reminded himself, "I will never be allowed outside again. Maybe never again as long as I live."

He turned and walked into the house, as silently as a shadow.

"Why?" he asked at the supper table that night. It wasn't a common question in the Garner house. There were plenty of "how's"—*How much rain'd the backfield get? How's the planting going?* Even "what's"—*What'd Matthew do with the five-sixteenth wrench? What's Dad going to do about that busted tire?* But "why" wasn't considered much worth asking. Luke asked again. "Why'd you have to sell the woods?"

Luke's dad harrumphed, and paused in the midst of shoveling forkfuls of boiled potatoes into his mouth.

"Told you before. We didn't have a choice. Government wanted it. You can't tell the Government no."

Mother came over and gave Luke's shoulder a reassuring squeeze before turning back to the stove. They had defied the Government once, with Luke. That had taken all the defiance they had in them. Maybe more.

"We wouldn't have sold the woods if we hadn't had to," she said, ladling out thick tomatoey soup. "The Government didn't ask *us* if we wanted houses there."

She pursed her lips as she slid the bowls of soup onto the table.

"But the Government's not going to live in the houses," Luke protested. At twelve, he knew better, but sometimes still pictured the Government as a very big, mean, fat person, two or three times as tall as an ordinary man, who went around yelling at people, "Not allowed!" and "Stop that!" It was because of the way his parents and older brothers talked: "Government won't let us plant corn there again." "Government's keeping the prices down." "Government's not going to like this crop."

"Probably some of the people who live in those houses

will be Government workers," Mother said. "It'll all be city people."

If he'd been allowed, Luke would have gone over to the kitchen window and peered out at the woods, trying for the umpteenth time to picture rows and rows of houses where the firs and maples and oaks now stood. Or had stood—Luke knew from a sneaked peek right before supper that half the trees were now toppled. Some already lay on the ground. Some hung at weird angles from their former lofty positions in the sky. Their absence made everything look different, like a fresh haircut exposing a band of untanned skin on a forehead. Even from deep inside the kitchen, Luke could tell the trees were missing because everything was brighter, more open. Scarier.

"And then, when those people move in, I have to stay away from the windows?" Luke asked, though he knew the answer.

The question made Dad explode. He slammed his hand down on the table.

"Then? You gotta stay away *now*! Everybody and his brother's going to be tramping around back there, to see what's going on. They see you—" He waved his fork violently. Luke wasn't sure what the gesture meant, but he knew it wasn't good.

No one had ever told him exactly what would happen if anyone saw him. Death? Death was what happened to the runt pigs who got stepped on by their stronger brothers and sisters. Death was a fly that stopped buzzing when the swatter hit it. He had a hard time thinking about himself in connection with the smashed fly or the dead pig, gone stiff in the sun. It made his stomach feel funny even trying.

"I don't think it's fair we've got to do Luke's chores now," Luke's other brother, Mark, grumbled. "Can't he go outside some? Maybe at night?"

Luke waited hopefully for the answer. But Dad just said, "No," without looking up.

"It's not fair," Mark said again. Mark was the second son—the lucky second, Luke thought when he was feeling sorry for himself. Mark was two years older than Luke and barely a year younger than Matthew, the oldest. Matthew and Mark were easily recognizable as brothers, with their dark hair and chiseled faces. Luke was fairer, smaller-boned, softer-looking. He often wondered if he'd ever look tougher, like them. Somehow he didn't think so.

"Luke don't do nothing nohow," Matthew jeered. "We won't miss his work at all."

"It's not my fault!" Luke protested. "I'd help more if—"

Mother laid her hands on his shoulders again. "Hush, all of you," she said. "Luke will do what he can. He always has."

The sound of tires on their gravel driveway came through the open window.

"Now, who—" Dad started. Luke knew the rest of the sentence. Who could that be? Why were they bothering him now, his first chance all day to sit down? It was a question Luke always heard the end of from the other side of a door. Today, skittish because of the woods coming down, he scrambled up faster than usual, dashing for the door to the back stairs. He knew without watching that Mother would take his plate from the table and hide it in a cupboard, would slide his chair back into the corner so it looked like an unneeded spare. In three seconds she would hide all evidence that Luke existed, just in time to step to the door and offer a weary smile to the fertilizer salesman or the Government inspector or whomever else had come to interrupt their supper.

CHAPTER TWO

There was a law against Luke.

Not him personally—everyone like him, kids who were born after their parents had already had two babies.

Actually, Luke didn't know if there was anyone else like him. He wasn't supposed to exist. Maybe he was the only one. They did things to women after they had their second baby, so they wouldn't have any more. And if there was a mistake, and a woman got pregnant anyway, she was supposed to get rid of it.

That was how Mother had explained it, years ago, the first and only time Luke had asked why he had to hide.

He had been six years old.

Before that, he had thought only very little kids had to stay out of sight. He had thought, as soon as he was as old as Matthew and Mark, he would get to go around like they did, riding to the backfield and even into town with Dad, hanging their heads and arms out the pickup window. He had thought, as soon as he got as old as Matthew and Mark, he could play in the front yard and kick the ball out into the road if he wanted. He had thought, as soon as he got as old as Matthew and Mark, he could go to school. They complained about it, whining, "Jeez, we gotta do homework!" and, "Who cares about spelling?" But they also talked about games at recess, and friends who shared candy at lunchtime or loaned them pocketknives to carve with.

Somehow, Luke never got as old as Matthew and Mark.

The day of his sixth birthday, Mother baked a cake, a special one with raspberry jam dripping down the sides. At supper that night she put six candles on the top and placed it in front of Luke and said, "Make a wish."

Staring into the ring of candles—proud that the number of his years finally made a ring, all around the cake—Luke suddenly remembered another cake, another ring of six candles. Mark's. He remembered Mark's sixth birthday. He remembered it because, even with the cake in front of him, Mark had been whining, "But I wanna have a party. Robert Joe had a party on his birthday. He got to have three friends over." Mother had said, "*Ssh*," and looked from Mark to Luke, saying something with her eyes that Luke didn't understand.

Startled by the memory, Luke let out his breath. Two of his candles flickered, and one went out. Matthew and Mark laughed.

"You ain't getting that wish," Mark said. "Baby. Can't even blow out candles."

Luke wanted to cry. He'd forgotten even to make a wish, and if he hadn't been surprised he would have been able to blow out all six candles. He knew he could have. And then he would have gotten—oh, he didn't know. A chance to ride to town in the pickup truck. A chance to play in the front yard. A chance to go to school. Instead, all he had was a strange memory that couldn't be right. Surely Luke was thinking about Mark's seventh birthday, or maybe his eighth. Mark couldn't have known Robert Joe when he was six, because he would have been hiding then, like Luke.

Luke thought about it for three days. He trailed along behind his mother as she hung wash out on the line, made strawberry preserves, scrubbed the bathroom floor. Several times he started to ask, "How old do I have to be before people can see me?" But something stopped him every time.

Finally, on the fourth day, after Dad, Matthew, and Mark scraped back their chairs from the breakfast table and headed out to the barn, Luke crouched by the kitchen's side window—one he wasn't supposed to look out because people driving by might catch a glimpse of his face. He tilted his head to the side and raised up just enough that his left eye was above the level of the windowsill. He watched Matthew and Mark running in the sunlight, the tops of their hog boots thumping against their knees. They were in full sight of the whole world, it seemed, and they didn't care. They were racing to the front door of the barn, not the side one off the backyard that Luke always had to use because it was hidden from the road.

Luke turned around and slid to the floor, out of sight.

"Matthew and Mark never had to hide, did they?" he asked.

Mother was scrubbing the remains of scrambled eggs out of the skillet. She turned her head and looked at him carefully.

"No," she said.

"Then why do I?"

She dried her hands and left the sink, something Luke had almost never seen her do if there were still dirty dishes left to be washed. She crouched beside him and smoothed his hair back from his forehead.

"Oh, Lukie, do you really need to know? Isn't it enough to know—things are just different for you?"

He thought about that. Mother was always saying he was the only one who would ever sit on her lap and cuddle. She still read bedtime stories to him, and he knew Matthew and Mark thought that was sissified. Was that what she meant? But he was just younger. He'd grow up. Wouldn't he be like them then?

With unusual stubbornness, Luke insisted, "I want to know why I'm different. I want to know why I have to hide."

So Mother told him.

Later, he wished he'd asked more questions. But at the time it was all he could do to listen to what she told him. He felt like he was drowning in the flow of her words.

"It just happened," she said. "You just happened. And we wanted you. I wouldn't even let your dad talk about... getting rid of you."

Luke pictured himself as a baby, left in a cardboard box

by the side of a road somewhere, the way Dad said people used to do with kittens, back when people were allowed to have pets. But maybe that wasn't what Mother meant.

"The Population Law hadn't been around long, then, and I had always wanted lots of kids. Before, I mean. Getting pregnant with you was like—a miracle. I thought the Government would get over their foolishness, maybe even by the time you were born, and then I'd have a new baby to show everyone."

"But you didn't," Luke managed to say. "You hid me."

His voice sounded strangely hoarse, like it belonged to someone else.

Mother nodded. "Once I started showing, I didn't go anywhere. That wasn't hard to do—where do I go, anyway? I didn't let Matthew and Mark leave the farm, for fear they'd say something. I didn't even say anything about you in letters to my mother and sister. I wasn't really scared then. It was just superstition. I didn't want to brag. I thought I'd go to the hospital to give birth. I wasn't going to keep you secret forever. But then..."

"Then what?" Luke asked.

Mother wouldn't look at him.

"Then they started running all that on TV about the Population Police, how the Population Police had ways of finding out everything, how they'd do anything to enforce the law."

Luke glanced toward the hulking television in the living room. He wasn't allowed to watch it. Was that why?

"And your dad started hearing rumors in town, about other babies…"

Luke shivered. Mother was looking far off into the distance, to where the rows of new corn plants met the horizon.

"I always wanted a John, too," she said. " 'Matthew, Mark, Luke, and John, bless the bed that I lie on.' But then I thank the Lord that I have you, at least. And it's worked out, the hiding, hasn't it?"

The smile she offered him was wobbly. He felt he had to help her.

"Yes," he said.

And somehow, after that, he didn't mind hiding so much anymore. Who wanted to meet strangers, anyway? Who wanted to go to school, where—if Matthew and Mark were to be believed—the teachers yelled, and the other boys would double-cross you if you didn't watch out? He was special. He was secret. He belonged at home—home, where his mother always let him have the first piece of apple pie because he was there and the other boys were away. Home, where he could cradle the new baby pigs in the barn, climb the trees at the edge of the woods, throw snowballs at the posts of the clothesline. Home, where the backyard always beckoned, always safe and protected by the house and the barn and the woods.

Until they took the woods away.

CHAPTER **THREE**

Luke lay on his stomach on the floor and idly ran the toy train back and forth on the track. The train had belonged to Dad when he was a little boy, and his own father before him. Luke could remember a time when his greatest longing had been for Mark to outgrow the train so Luke could have it all to himself. But it wasn't what he wanted to play with today. There was a beautiful day unfolding outside, with fleecy clouds in a blue, blue sky, and a mild breeze rustling the grass in the backyard. He hadn't left the house in a week now, and he could almost hear the outdoors calling to him. But now he wasn't even allowed in the same room as an uncovered window.

"Are you *trying* to be discovered?" Dad had bellowed at Luke just that morning, when he'd held the shade a few inches back from the kitchen window and peeked out longingly.

Luke jumped. He'd been so busy thinking about running barefoot through the grass that he'd half-forgotten there was anyone or anything behind him, in the house.

"No one's out there," he said, glancing again to be sure.

He'd been trying not to look beyond the ragged edge of the backyard to the bulldozed mess of branches, trunks, leaves, and mud that had once been his beloved woods.

"Yeah?" Dad said. "Did it ever occur to you that if there is, they might see you before you see them?"

He grabbed Luke by the arm and jerked him back a good three feet. Freed from Luke's grasp, the bottom of the shade banged against the windowsill.

"You can't look out at all," Dad said. "I mean it. From now on, just stay away from the windows. And don't go into a room unless we've got the shades or curtains pulled."

"But then I can't see anything," Luke protested.

"Better that than to get turned in," Dad said.

Dad sounded like he might feel sorry for Luke, but that only made things worse. Luke turned around and left, scared he might cry in front of Dad.

Now he gave the toy train a shove, and it careened off the track. It landed upside down, wheels spinning.

"Who cares?" Luke muttered.

There was a harsh knock on his door.

"Population Police! Open up!"

Luke didn't move.

"That's not funny, Mark!" he shouted.

Mark opened the door and bounded up the stairs that led to Luke's room proper. Luke's room was also the attic, a fact he had never minded. Mother long ago had shoved all the trunks and boxes as far as they could go under the eaves, leaving prime space for Luke's brass bed and circular rag rug and books and toys. Luke had even heard Matthew and Mark grumble about Luke having the biggest room. But they had windows.

"Scared you this time, didn't I?" Mark asked.

"No," Luke said. Nothing would force him to admit that his heart had jumped. Mark had been playing the "Population Police" joke for years, always out of their parents' earshot. Usually Luke just ignored Mark, but now, with Dad acting so skittish...What would Luke have done if it really had been the Population Police? What would they do to him?

"Matt and me, we've never told anyone about you," Mark said, suddenly serious, which was strange for him. "And you know Mother and Dad don't say anything. You're good at hiding. So you're safe, you know?"

"I know," Luke muttered.

Mark kicked the toy train Luke had crashed. "Still playing with baby toys?" he asked, as if to make up for slipping and being nice.

Luke shrugged. Normally, he wouldn't have wanted Mark to know he played with the train anymore. But today everything else was so bad that that didn't matter.

"Did you come up here just to bug me?" Luke asked.

Mark put on an offended look.

"Thought you might want to play checkers," he said.

Luke squinted.

"Mother told you to, right?" he asked.

"No."

"You're lying," Luke said, not caring how nasty he sounded.

"Well, if you're going to be that way—"

"Just leave me alone, okay?"

"Okay, okay." Mark backed down the stairs. "Jeez!"

Alone again, Luke felt a little sorry he'd been so mean. Maybe Mark had told the truth. Luke should apologize. But he didn't really feel like it.

Luke got up and started pacing his room. The squeak of the third board in from the stairs annoyed him. He hated having to duck under the rafters on the far side of his bed. Even his favorite model cars, lined up on the shelves in the corner, bothered him today. Why should he have model cars? He'd never even sat in a real one. He never would. He'd never get to do anything or go anywhere. He might as well just rot up here in the attic. He'd thought about that before, on the rare occasions when Mother, Dad, Matthew, and Mark all went somewhere and left him behind—what if something happened to them and they never came back? Would someone find him years from now, abandoned and dead? He'd read a story in one of the old books in the attic about a bunch of kids finding a deserted pirate ship, and then a skeleton in one of the rooms. He'd be like that skeleton. And now that he wasn't allowed in rooms with uncovered windows, he'd be a skeleton in the dark.

Luke looked up automatically, as if to remind himself that nothing lit the rafters but the single bulb over his head. Except—there was light at either end of the ceiling, leaking in under the peak of the roof.

Luke stood up and went to investigate. Of course. He should have remembered. There were vents at each end of the roof. Dad grumbled occasionally about heating the attic for Luke—"It's just like throwing money out those vents"—but Mother always fixed him with one of her stares, and nothing changed.

Now Luke climbed on top of one of the largest trunks and looked down through the vent. He could see out! He could see a strip of the road and the cornfield beyond, its leaves waving in the breeze. The vent slanted down and limited his view, but at least he was sure nobody would ever be able to see him.

For a moment, Luke was excited, but that quickly faded. He didn't want to spend the rest of his life watching the corn grow. Without much hope, he stepped down from the trunk and went to the other end of the attic, the portion that faced the backyard. He had to slide boxes around and drag an old step stool from the opposite end of the attic, but finally his eyes were level with the back vent.

The view was not of the backyard—it was too close— but of the former woods. He'd never realized it before, but the land there sloped away from his family's house, so he had a clear view of acres and acres that once had been covered with trees. The land was abuzz with activity now. Huge yellow bulldozers shoved brush back from a rough road that had been traced out with gravel. Other vehicles

Luke couldn't identify were digging holes for huge concrete pipes. Luke watched in fascination. He knew tractors and combines, of course, and had seen his dad's bush hog and manure spreader and gravity wagons up close, in the barn. But these machines were different, designed for different jobs. And they were all operated by different people.

Once, when Luke was younger, a tramp had walked up to the house and Luke had only had time to hide under the sink in the mudroom before the man was in the house, begging for food. The door of the cabinet was cracked, so Luke had been able to peek out and see the man's patched trousers and holey shoes. He'd heard his whiny voice: "I ain't got no job, and I ain't et in three days…. No, no, I can't do no farmwork for my food. What do you think I am? I'm sick. I'm starving…."

Other than that tramp and pictures in books, Luke had never seen another human being besides his parents and Matthew and Mark. He'd never dreamed there was such variety.

Many of the people running the bulldozers and shovel contraptions were stripped of their shirts, while others standing nearby even wore ties and coats. Some were fat and some were thin; some were browned by the sun and some were paler than Luke himself, who would never be tan again. They were all moving—shifting gears and lowering pipe, waving others into position or, at the very least, talking at full speed. All that activity made Luke dizzy. The pictures in books always showed people still.

Overwhelmed, Luke closed his eyes, then opened them again for fear of missing something.

"Luke?"

Reluctantly, Luke slid down from his step stool perch and scrambled over to recline innocently on his bed.

"Come in," he called to his mother.

She climbed the stairs heavily.

"You okay?"

Luke dangled his feet over the side of the bed.

"Sure. I'm fine."

Mother sat on the bed beside him and patted his leg.

"It's—" she swallowed hard. "It's not easy, the life you've got to live. I know you'd like to look outside. You'd like to go outside—"

"That's okay, Mother," Luke said. He could have told her then about the vents—he didn't see how anyone could object to him looking out there—but something stopped him. What if they took that away from him, too? What if Mother told Dad, and Dad said, "No, no, that's too much of a risk. I forbid it"? Luke wouldn't be able to stand it. He kept silent.

Mother ruffled his hair.

"You're a trooper," she said. "I knew you'd hold up all right."

Luke leaned against his mother's arm, and she moved her arm around his shoulders and hugged him tight to her side. He felt a little guilty for keeping a secret, but mostly reassured—loved and reassured.

Then, more to herself than to him, Mother added, "And things could be worse."

Somehow, that wasn't comforting. Luke didn't know why, but he had a feeling what she really meant was that things were going to get worse. He snuggled tighter against Mother, hoping he was wrong.

CHAPTER *FOUR*

Luke found out what Mother meant a few days later when he came down for breakfast. As usual, he opened the door from the back stairs to the kitchen only a crack. He could remember barely a handful of times in his entire life when someone had dropped by before breakfast, and each time Mother had managed to send Matthew or Mark up to warn Luke to stay out of sight. But he always checked. Today he could see Dad and Matthew and Mark at the table, and knew from the sound of frying bacon that Mother must be at the stove.

"Are the shades closed?" he called softly.

Mother opened the door to the stairs. Luke started to step into the kitchen, but she put out her arm to keep him back. She handed him a plate full of scrambled eggs and bacon.

"Luke, honey? Can you eat sitting on the bottom step there?"

"What?" Luke asked.

Mother looked beseechingly over her shoulder.

"Dad thinks—I mean, it's not safe anymore to have you

in the kitchen. You can still eat with us, and talk to us and all, but you'll be…over here."

She waved her hand toward the stairs behind Luke.

"But with the shades pulled—" Luke started.

"One of those workers asked me yesterday, 'Hey, farmer, you got air-conditioning in that house of yours?'" Dad said from the table. He didn't turn around. He didn't seem to want to look at Luke. "We keep the shades pulled, hot day like today, people get suspicious. This way is safer. I'm sorry."

And then Dad did turn around and glance at Luke, once. Luke tried to keep from looking upset.

"So what'd you tell him?" Matthew asked, as if the worker's question was only a matter of curiosity.

"Told him of course we don't have air-conditioning. Farming don't make nobody a millionaire."

Dad took a long sip of coffee.

"Okay, Luke?" Mother asked.

"Yes," he mumbled. He took the plate of eggs and bacon, but it didn't look good to him now. He knew every bite he ate would stick in his throat. He sat down on the step, out of sight of both kitchen windows.

"We'll leave the door open," Mother said. She hovered over him, as if unwilling to return to the stove. "This isn't too much different, is it?"

"Mother—" Dad said warningly.

Through the open windows, Luke could hear the rumble of several trucks and cars. The workers had arrived for the day. He knew from watching through the vent the past few days that the caravan of vehicles came up the road like a parade. The cars would peel off to the side and unload the nicer dressed men. The more rugged vehicles pulled on in to the muddiest sections, and the people inside would scatter to the bulldozers and backhoes that had been left outside overnight. But the vehicles barely had time to get cold, because the workers were there now from sunup to sundown. Someone was in a hurry for them to finish.

"Luke—I'm sorry," Mother said, and scurried back to the stove. She loaded a plate for herself, then sat down at the table, beside Luke's usual spot. His chair wasn't even in the kitchen anymore.

For a while, Luke watched Dad, Mother, Matthew, and Mark eating in silence, a complete family of four. Once, he cleared his throat, ready to protest again. *You can't do this— it's not fair—* Then he choked back the words, unspoken. They were only trying to protect him. What could he do?

Resolutely, Luke stuck his fork in the pile of scrambled eggs on his plate and took a bite. He ate the whole plateful of food without tasting any of it.

CHAPTER *FIVE*

L uke ate every meal after that on the bottom step. It became a habit, but a hated one. He had never noticed before, but Mother often spoke too softly to be heard from any distance, and Matthew and Mark always made their nasty comments under their breath. So they would start laughing, often at Luke's expense, and he couldn't defend himself because he didn't know what they had said. He couldn't even hear Mother saying, "Now, be nice, boys." After a week or two, a lot of the time, he didn't even try to listen to the rest of the family's conversation.

But even he was curious the hot July day when the letter arrived about the pigs.

Matthew brought the mail in that day from the mailbox at the crossroads a mile away. (Luke had never seen them, of course, but Matthew and Mark had told him there were three mailboxes there, one for each of the families that lived on their road.) Usually the Garners' mail was just bills or thin envelopes carrying curt orders from the Government about how much corn to plant, which fertilizer to use, and where to take their crop when it was harvested. A letter from a relative was a cause to celebrate, and Mother always dropped whatever she was doing and sat down to open it with trembling hands, calling out at intervals, "Oh, Aunt Effie's in the hospital again...." or, "Tsk, Lisabeth's going to marry that fellow after all...." Luke almost felt he knew his relatives, though they lived hundreds of miles away. And, of course, they didn't even know he existed. The letters Mother wrote back, painstakingly, late at night, when she'd saved up enough money for a stamp, contained plenty of news of Matthew and Mark, but never once had mentioned Luke's name.

This letter was as thick as some from Luke's grandmother, but it bore an official seal, and the return address was an embossed DEPARTMENT OF HUMAN HABITATION, ENVIRONMENTAL STANDARDS DIVISION. Matthew held the letter at arm's length, the way Luke had seen him hold dead baby pigs when they had to be carried out of the barn.

Dad looked worried the minute he saw the letter in Matthew's hand. Matthew put the letter down beside Dad's silverware. Dad sighed.

"Can't be anything but bad news," Dad said. "No use ruining a good meal. It can wait."

He went back to eating chicken and dumplings. Only after his last belch did he turn the envelope over and run a dirt-rimmed fingernail under the flap. He unfolded the letter.

" 'It has come to our attention…,' " he read aloud. "Well, so far I understand it." Then he read silently for a while, calling out at intervals, "Mother, what's 'offal'?" and, "Where's that dictionary? Matthew, look up 'reciprocity.' " Finally, he threw down the whole thick packet and proclaimed, "They're going to make us get rid of our hogs."

"What?" Matthew asked. More serious than Mark, he had talked for as long as anyone could remember about, "When I get my own farm, it's going to be all hogs. I'll make the Government let me do that, somehow…." Now he looked over Dad's shoulder. "You mean they're just going to make us sell a lot at one time, right? But we can build the herd back up—"

"Nope," Dad said. "Those people in them fancy new houses won't be able to stand pig smell. So we can't raise hogs no more." He threw the letter out into the center of the table for all to see. "What'd they expect, building next to a farm?"

From his seat on the stairs, Luke had to hold himself back from going to fish the edge of the letter out of the chicken gravy and looking at it himself.

"They can't do that, can they?" he asked.

Nobody answered. Nobody needed to. Luke felt like a fool for asking as soon as the words were out of his mouth. For once, he was glad of his hiding place.

Mother twisted a dishrag in her hand.

"Those hogs are our bread and butter," she said. "With

grain prices the way they are...what are we going to live on?"

Dad just looked at her. After a moment, so did Matthew and Mark. Luke didn't know why.

CHAPTER SIX

The tax bill arrived two weeks later, the day that Dad, Matthew, and Mark loaded the hogs onto the livestock trailer and took them all away. Most were going to the slaughterhouse. The ones too young and too small to bring a decent price were going to an auction for feeder pigs. Luke watched through the vent at the front of the house as Dad drove by in the battered pickup with each load. Matthew and Mark sat in the back of the pickup, making sure the trailer stayed hitched right. Even three stories up, Luke could see Matthew's hangdog expression.

Then when the three of them came into the house for dinner, after washing the last of the hog smell off their hands in the mudroom, Dad handed Mother the tax bill without comment. She put down the wooden spoon she'd been using to stir the stew and unfolded the letter. Then she dropped it.

"Why, that's—" she seemed to be doing the math in her head as she bent to retrieve it. "That's three times what it usually is. There must be a mistake."

Dad shook his head grimly. "No mistake. I talked to Williker at the auction."

The Willikers were their nearest neighbors, with a house three miles down the road. Luke always pictured them with monster scales and fierce claws because of the number of times he'd been cautioned, "You don't want the Willikers to see you."

Dad went on. "Williker says they raised everyone's taxes because of them fancy houses. Makes our land worth more."

"Isn't that good?" Luke asked eagerly. It was strange— he should hate the new houses for replacing his woods and forcing him to stay indoors. But he'd half-fallen in love with them, having watched every foundation poured, every wooden skeleton of walls and roofs raised to the sky. They were his main entertainment, aside from talking to Mother when she came upstairs for what she called "my Luke breaks." Sometimes she pretended his room needed cleaning as badly as the bread needed baking or the garden needed weeding. Sometimes she just sat and talked.

Dad was shaking his head in disgust over Luke's question.

"No. It's only good if we're selling. And we ain't. All it means for us is that the Government thinks they can get more money out of us."

Matthew was slumped in his chair at the table. "How are we going to pay?" he asked. "That's more than we got for all the hogs, and that was supposed to carry us through for a long time—"

Dad didn't answer. Even Mark, who normally had a smart-alecky comeback for everything, was stupefied.

Mother had turned back to her stew.

"I got my work permit today," she said softly. "The factory's hiring. If I get on there, I can maybe get an advance on my paycheck."

Luke's jaw dropped.

"You can't go to work," he said. "Who will—" He wanted to say, *Who will stay with me? Who will I talk to all day when everyone else is outside?* But that seemed too selfish. Luke looked around. No one else looked surprised by Mother's news. He shut his mouth.

CHAPTER SEVEN

By mid-September, Luke's days had fallen into a familiar pattern. He got up at dawn just for the chance to sit on the stairs and watch the rest of his family eat breakfast. They all rushed now. Mother had to be at the factory by seven. Dad was trying to get all the machinery in working order before harvest. And Matthew and Mark were back in school. Only Luke had time to linger over his undercooked bacon and dry toast. He didn't bother asking for butter because that meant someone would have to stand up and bring it over to him, all the while pretending for the sake of the open window that they'd just forgotten something upstairs.

As soon as the rest of his family had stomped out the door, Luke went back to his room and watched out the vents—first out the front, to see Matthew and Mark climb onto the school bus, then out the back, where the new houses were practically finished. They were mansions, as large as the Garners' house and barn put together. They gleamed in the morning sunlight as though their walls were studded with precious jewels. For all Luke knew, maybe they were.

Hordes of workmen still arrived every morning, but almost all of them worked indoors now. They headed into the houses first thing, carrying rolls of carpet, stacks of drywall, cans of paint. Luke couldn't see much of them after that. He spent more time now watching a new kind of traffic: expensive-looking cars driving slowly down the newly paved streets. Sometimes they pulled into a driveway and went into one of the houses, usually trailing a woman who appeared to be talking nonstop. It had taken Luke a while to figure it out—he certainly hadn't dared ask anyone else in his family—but he thought maybe the people were thinking about buying the houses. Once he realized that, he studied each potential neighbor carefully. He'd overheard Mother and Dad marveling that the people moving into the new houses were not just going to be city people, but Barons. Barons were unbelievably rich, Luke knew. They had things ordinary people hadn't had in years. Luke wasn't sure how the Barons had gotten rich, when everybody else was poor. But Dad never said the word "Baron" without a curse word or two in front of it.

The people streaming through the houses did look different from anyone in Luke's family. They were mostly thin, beautiful women in formfitting dresses, and heavyset men in what Luke's dad and brothers called sissy clothes—shiny shoes and clean, dressy pants and jackets. Luke always felt a little embarrassed for them, showing up like that. Or maybe he was embarrassed for his family, that they never looked like any of the Barons. Luke preferred it when the adults had children with them and he could concentrate on them. The smallest ones were always as dressed up as their parents, with hair bows and suspenders and other geegaws Luke knew his parents would never buy. The older kids usually seemed to be wearing whatever they'd grabbed first out of their closet that morning.

Though he knew no one would dare show up with three kids, he always counted: "One, two..." "One..." "One, two..."

What if a family with just one kid moved in behind them, and he sneaked into their house and pretended to be their second child? He could go to school, go to town, act like Matthew and Mark....

What a joke—Luke living with Barons. More likely he'd be shot for trespassing. Or turned in.

When he began thinking things like that, he always jumped down from his perch by the vent and grabbed a book from one of the dusty stacks by the eaves. Mother had taught him to read and do math, as much as she knew herself. "At least we have a few books for you...," she often mumbled sadly when she left in the morning. He'd read all their books dozens of times, even the ones with titles like *Diseases of the Porcine Species* and *Common Grasses of Our Countryside*. His favorites were the handful of adventure books, the ones that let him pretend he was a knight fighting a dragon to rescue a kidnapped princess, or an explorer sailing on the high seas, holding tight to a mast while a hurricane raged about him.

He liked to forget he was Luke Garner, third child hidden in the attic.

Sometime around noon he'd hear the door from the mudroom to the kitchen swing open and he'd go down and eat at the same time as his dad. Without Mother there were no homemade pies now, no mashed potatoes, no roasts that sent good smells throughout the house. Dad always made four sandwiches, checked to make sure no one could see him, then handed two of them to Luke in the stairwell.

Dad never talked—he'd explained that he didn't want anyone overhearing him, and wondering. But he did turn the radio on for the noon farm report, and there was usually a song or two after that before Dad silenced the radio and went outside to work again.

When Dad left, Luke went back to his room to read or watch the houses again.

At six-thirty Mother came home, and she always stopped in and said hi to Luke before rushing out to do a whole day's work in the few hours before bedtime. Usually Matthew or Mark came up to visit him, too, but they could never stay long, either. They had to help Dad before supper, then do homework afterwards. And they always had been nicest to Luke outdoors. Before the woods came down, the three of them often had played kickball or football or spud in the backyard, after school and chores. Matthew and Mark always fought about who got to have Luke on his team, because, even if Luke wasn't very good, two boys together could always beat the third.

Now they played halfhearted games of cards or checkers with Luke, but Luke could tell they'd rather be outside.

So would he.

He tried not to think about it.

The best part of the day came at the end, when Mother tucked him in. She'd be relaxed then. She'd stay for an hour sometimes, asking him what he'd read that day, or telling him stories about the factory.

Then one night, when she was telling how her plastic glove had gotten stuck in a chicken she'd de-gutted that day, Mother suddenly stopped in the middle of a sentence.

"Mother?" Luke said.

She answered with a snore. She'd fallen asleep sitting up.

Luke studied her face, seeing lines of fatigue that hadn't been there before, noticing that the hair around her face now held as much gray as brown.

"Mother?" he said again, gently shaking her arm.

She jerked. "—but I cleaned that chicken al— oh. Sorry, Luke. You need tucking in, don't you?"

She fluffed his pillow, smoothed his sheet.

Luke sat up. "That's okay, Mother. I'm getting too old for this any"—he swallowed a lump in his throat— "anyway. I bet you weren't still tucking Matthew or Mark in when they were twelve."

"No," she said quietly.

"Then I don't need it, either."

"Okay," she said.

She kissed his forehead, anyhow, then turned out the light. Luke turned his face to the wall until she left.

CHAPTER *EIGHT*

One cool, rainy morning a few weeks later, Luke's family left in such a rush, they barely had time to say good-bye. They dashed out the door after breakfast, Matthew and Mark complaining about their packed lunches, Dad calling back, "I'm going to that auction up at Chytlesville. Won't be home until supper." Mother hurried back and handed Luke a bag of cracklings and three pears and some biscuits from the night before. She muttered, "So you won't get hungry," and gave him a quick kiss on the head. Then she was gone, too.

Luke peeked around the stairway door, surveying the chaos of dirty pans and crumb-covered plates left in the kitchen. He knew not to look out as far as the window, but he did, anyway. His heart gave a strange jump when he saw the window was covered. Someone must have pulled the shade the night before, to try to keep the kitchen warm, and then forgotten to raise it in the morning. Luke dared to lean out a little further—yes, the shade was down on the other window, too. For the first time in almost six months, he could step out into the kitchen and not worry about being seen. He could run, skip, jump—dance, even—on the vast linoleum without fear. He could clean up the kitchen and surprise Mother. He could do anything.

He put his right foot out, tentatively, not quite daring to put his full weight on it. The floor squeaked. He froze. Nothing happened, but he retreated, anyway. He went back up the stairs, crawled along the second-floor hallway to avoid the windows, then climbed the stairs to the attic. He was so disgusted with himself, he could taste it.

I am a coward. I am a chicken. I deserve to be locked away in the attic forever, ran through his head. *No, no*, he countered himself, *I'm cautious. I'm making a plan.*

He climbed up onto the stool on top of a trunk that served as his perch for watching out the back vents. The neighborhood behind his house was fully occupied now. He knew all the families and had come up with names for most of them. The Big Car Family had four expensive cars sitting in their driveway. The Gold Family all had hair the color of sunshine. The Birdbrain Family had set a row of thirty birdhouses along their backyard fence, even though Luke could have told them it was pointless to do that until spring. The house he could see best, right behind the Garners' backyard, was occupied by the Sports Family. Two teenaged boys lived there, and their deck overflowed with soccer balls, baseball bats, tennis rackets, basketballs, hockey sticks, and apparatus from games Luke could only guess at.

Today, he wasn't interested in games. He was interested in seeing the families leave.

He had noticed before that all of the houses were empty by nine in the morning, with kids off to school and grown-ups off to work. Three or four of the women didn't seem to have jobs, but they left, too, returning late in the afternoon with shopping bags. Today, he just had to make sure no one was staying home sick.

The Gold Family left first, two blond heads in one car, two blond heads in another. The Sports Family was next, the boys carrying football pads and helmets, their mother teetering on high heels. Then there was a flurry of cars streaming from every driveway onto the still-sparkling new streets. Luke counted each person, keeping track so carefully that he made scratches on the wall, and counted the scratches twice again at the end. Yes—twenty-eight people gone. He was safe.

Luke scrambled down from his chair, his head spinning with plans. First, he'd clean up the kitchen; then he'd start some bread for supper. He'd never made bread before, but he'd watched Mother a million times. Then maybe he could pull the shades in the rest of the house and clean it thoroughly. He couldn't vacuum—that'd be too loud—but he could dust and scrub and polish. Mother would be so pleased. Then, in the afternoon, before Matthew or Mark or the kids in the neighborhood got back, he could put something on for supper. Maybe potato soup. Why, he could do this every day. He'd never considered housework or cooking particularly thrilling before—Matthew and Mark always scoffed at it as women's work—but it was better than nothing. And maybe, just maybe, if this worked, he could convince Dad to let him sneak out to the barn and help there, too.

Luke was so excited, he stepped into the kitchen without a second thought this time. Who cared if the floor creaked? No one was there to hear it. He gathered up dishes from the table and piled them into the sink, scrubbing everything with extraordinary zeal. He measured out flour and lard and milk and yeast and was putting it all in a bowl when it occurred to him it might be okay to turn on the radio, very softly. Nobody'd hear. And if they did, they'd just figure the family had forgotten to turn it off, just as they'd forgotten to raise the shades.

The bread was in the oven and Luke was picking up lint by hand from the living room rug when he heard tires on the gravel driveway. It was two o'clock in the afternoon, too early for the school bus or Mother or Dad. Luke sprinted for the stairs, hoping whoever it was would just go away.

No luck. He heard the side door creaking open, then Dad exclaiming, "What the—"

He was back early. That shouldn't matter. But hiding on the staircase, Luke suddenly felt like the radio was as loud as an entire orchestra, like the smell of baking bread could fill three counties.

"Luke!" Dad yelled.

Luke heard his father's hand on the doorknob. He opened the door.

"I was just trying to help," Luke blubbered. "I was safe. You left the shades down, so I thought it was okay, and I made sure everyone was gone from the neighborhood, and—"

Dad glared. "You can't be sure," he snapped. "People like that—they get deliveries all the time, they get sick and come home from work, they have maids come during the day—"

Luke could have protested, no, the maids never come before the kids get home from school. But he didn't want to give himself away any more than he already had.

"The shades were down," he said. "I didn't turn on a single light. Even if there were a thousand people back there, nobody would know I was here! Please—I've just got to do something. Look, I made bread, and cleaned up, and—"

"What if a Government inspector or someone had stopped by here?"

"I would have hidden. Like always."

Dad was shaking his head. "And leave them smelling bread baking in an empty house? You don't seem to understand," he said. "You can't take any chances. You can't. Because—"

At that precise moment, the buzzer on the oven went off, sounding as loud as a siren. Dad gave Luke a dirty look and stalked over to the oven. He pulled out the two bread pans and tossed them on the stove top. He flipped off the radio.

"I don't want you in the kitchen again," he said. "You stay hidden. That's an order."

He went out the door without looking back.

Luke fled up the stairs. He wanted to stomp, angrily, but he couldn't. No noise allowed. In his room, he hesitated, too upset to read, too restless to do anything else. He kept hearing *You stay hidden. That's an order,* echoing in his ears. But he'd been hidden. He'd been careful. To prove his point—to himself, at least—he climbed back up on his perch by the back vents and looked out on the quiet neighborhood.

All the driveways were empty. Nothing moved, not even the flag on the Gold Family's flagpole or the spokes on the Birdbrain Family's fake windmill. And then, out of the corner of his eye, Luke caught a glimpse of something behind one window of the Sports Family's house.

A face. A child's face. In a house where two boys already lived.

CHAPTER NINE

L uke was so surprised, he lost his balance and almost fell backwards off the trunk. By the time he recovered and righted himself, the face was gone. Had he imagined it? Was it just one of the Sports Family brothers home early from school? Kids got sick, like Dad said, or they decided to play hooky. Luke tried to remember every detail of the face he'd seen, or thought he'd seen. It had been younger than either of the Sports Family brothers'. Softer. Hadn't it?

Maybe it was a thief. Or a maid, come early.

No. It had been a child. A—

He didn't even let himself think what another child in that house would be.

He stared for hours at the Sports Family's house, but no face reappeared. Nothing happened until six, when the two Sports Family boys drove in in their jeep, unloaded their football gear, and carried it into the house. They didn't run out screaming about being robbed.

And he'd seen no thief leave. He'd seen no maid leave.

At six-thirty, Luke reluctantly climbed down from his

perch when he heard his mother's knock on the door. He sat down on his bed and muttered a distracted, "Come in."

She rushed to hug him.

"Luke—I'm sorry. I know you were just trying to help. And everything is amazingly clean. I'd love it if you could do this every day. But your father thinks—I mean, you can't—"

Luke was so busy thinking about the face in the window that at first he couldn't figure out what she was talking about. Oh. The bread. The housecleaning. The radio.

"That's okay," Luke mumbled.

But it wasn't, and it never would be. His anger came back. Why did his parents have to be so careful? Why didn't they just lock him in one of the trunks in the attic and be done with it?

"Can't you talk to him?" Luke asked. "Can't you convince him—"

Mother pushed Luke's hair back from his face. "I'll try," she said. "But you know he's just trying to protect you. We can't take any chances."

Even if the face in the window of the Sports Family house was another third child, so what? Luke and the other kid could live right next door all their lives and never meet. Luke might never see the other kid again. And he'd certainly never see Luke.

Luke lowered his head.

"What am I supposed to do?" he asked. "There's nothing

for me to do. Am I supposed to just sit in this room the rest of my life?"

Mother was stroking his hair now. It made him feel itchy and irritable.

"Oh, Lukie," she said. "You can do so much. Read and play and sleep whenever you want…. Believe me, I'd like to live a day of your life right about now."

"No you wouldn't," Luke muttered, but he said it so softly, he was sure Mother couldn't hear. He knew she wouldn't understand.

If there was a third child in the Sports Family, would he understand? Did he feel the way Luke did?

CHAPTER *TEN*

When Luke went down to supper, he saw that Mother had set his two loaves of bread out on the china plate she used for holidays and special occasions. She was showing off the bread the way she used to tape up the crooked drawings Matthew and Mark brought home from school when they were little. But something had gone wrong—maybe Luke hadn't used enough yeast, or he'd kneaded the dough too much or too little—and the loaves had turned out flat. They looked lopsided and pathetic in the center of the table.

Luke wished Mother had just thrown them away.

"It's cold out now. Nobody'd notice if you pulled the shades. Why can't I sit at the table with all of you?" he asked when he reached the bottom of the stairs.

"Oh, Luke—" Mother started.

"Someone might see your shadow through the shade," Dad said.

"They wouldn't know it was mine," Luke said.

"But there'd be five. Someone might get suspicious," Mother said patiently. "Luke, we're just trying to protect you. How about a big slice of your bread? There's cold beef and canned beans, too."

Resignedly, Luke sat down on the stairs.

Matthew asked about the auction Dad had gone to.

"I drove all that way for nothing," Dad said disgustedly. "I waited four hours for the tractors to come up, and then I couldn't even afford the first bid."

"At least you got home in time to fix that back fence before dark," Mother said, cutting the bread.

And yell at me, Luke thought bitterly. What was wrong with him? Nothing had changed. Except he'd maybe seen a face that maybe belonged to someone like him—

Matthew and Mark suddenly noticed the bread Mother was doling out.

"What's wrong with that?" Mark asked.

"I'm sure it will taste fine," Mother said. "It's Luke's first try."

Luke muttered, "And my last," too softly for anyone to hear. There were advantages to sitting on the other side of the room from everyone else.

"Luke made bread?" Mark said incredulously. "Yuck."

"Yeah. And I put special poison in one of the loaves, that only affects fourteen-year-olds," Luke said. He pantomimed death, clutching his hands around his own neck, letting his tongue hang out of his mouth, and lolling his head to the side. "If you're nice to me, I'll tell you which loaf is safe."

That shut Mark up but earned Luke a frown from

Mother. Luke felt strange about the joke, anyway. Of course he'd never poison anyone, but—if something happened to Matthew or Mark, would Luke have to hide anymore? Would he become the public second son, free to go to town and to school and everywhere else that Matthew and Mark went? Could his parents find some way to explain a "new" child already twelve years old?

It wasn't something Luke could ask. He felt guilty just thinking about it.

Mark was making a big ceremony out of bringing the bread to his mouth.

"I'm not scared of you," he taunted, and took a big bite. He swallowed with great difficulty and pretended to gag. "Water, water—quick!" He gulped down half his glass and glared at Luke. "Tastes like poison, all right."

Luke bit into his bread. It was dry and crumbly and tasteless, not like Mother's at all. And everybody knew it. Even Dad and Mother had pained expressions on their faces as they chewed. Dad finally pushed his slice away.

"That's okay, Luke," he said. "I'm not sure I'd want any son of mine getting too good at baking, anyhow. That's what a man gets married for."

Matthew and Mark guffawed.

"Getting married soon, Luke?" Mark teased.

"Sure," Luke said, struggling to sound as devil-may-care as Mark. "But don't think I'd invite *you* to the wedding."

He felt a cold, hard lump in his stomach that wasn't the

bread. Of course he'd never get married. Or do anything. He'd never leave the house.

Mark switched to teasing Matthew, who evidently did have a girlfriend. Luke watched the rest of his family laughing.

"May I be excused?" Luke asked.

Everyone turned to him in surprise. Usually he was the last one to make that request. Mother often begged Matthew and Mark, "Can't you wait, and talk to Luke a little bit longer?"

"Done already?" Mother asked.

"I'm not very hungry," Luke said.

Mother gave him a worried look but nodded, anyway.

Luke went to his room and climbed onto the stool by the back vents. In the dark, it was easier than ever to see into the houses of the new neighborhood. Their windows were lit up against the night. Some families were eating, like his. He could see one set of four people around a dining room table, and one set of three. Some families had their curtains or shades drawn, but sometimes the material was thin and he could still see shadows of the people inside.

Only the Sports Family had all their windows totally blocked, covered by heavy blinds.

CHAPTER *ELEVEN*

Luke watched the Sports Family house constantly after that. Before, he had just looked out the back vents in the early morning and late afternoon, when he knew people were about. But he'd seen the face at two o'clock. Maybe the other kid knew the rhythms of the neighborhood, too, and let his guard down only during times he considered safe.

For three long days, Luke saw nothing.

Then on the fourth day, he was rewarded: One panel of one of the blinds on an upstairs window flipped quickly up and down at eleven o'clock.

The seventh day the blinds in a downstairs window were left up in the morning. Luke saw a light go on and off at 9:07, two full hours after the last of the Sports Family had left. A half hour later, the Sports Family mother drove in in her red car and stomped into the house. Two minutes later, the blind in the downstairs window went down. The mother left immediately.

The thirteenth day was unseasonably warm, and Luke sweated in his attic. Some of the Sports Family's windows were left open, though still covered by the blinds. The wind blew the blinds back a couple times. Luke saw lights on in some of the rooms some of the time, in other rooms as the day wore on. Once he even thought he saw a glow of a TV screen.

He had no doubts anymore. Someone was hiding in the Sports Family house.

The question was, what could he do about it?

CHAPTER TWELVE

Harvest came. Matthew and Mark stayed out of school to help Dad bring the crops in, the three of them working some days from dawn until midnight. Mother's factory got busier, too, and she began working two or three hours of overtime every day. She brought up a store of food to Luke's room so he wouldn't get hungry while they were all away.

"There!" she said cheerfully, lining up boxes of crackers and bags of fruit. "This way, you won't even miss us."

Her eyes begged him not to complain.

"Uh-huh," he said, trying to sound game. "I'll be fine."

He watched the Sports Family house only sporadically now. What other proof did he need? What good did it do him to know about the other third child? What did he expect—that the other kid would run out in his backyard and yell, "Hey, Luke, come out and play!"?

He munched his solitary apples. He ate his crackers alone.

And in spite of himself, a crazy idea grew in his mind, sprouting new details daily.

What if he sneaked into the Sports Family house and met the other third child?

He could do it. It was possible. Theoretically.

He spent entire days plotting his route. He'd be hidden by bushes and the barn through much of his yard. It was only about six feet from there to the nearest tree in the Sports Family's backyard. He could crawl on his stomach. Then he'd be hidden by the fence the Sports Family shared with the Birdbrain Family—all those birdhouses might actually help. After that, it was only three steps to the Sports Family house. They had a sliding-glass door at the back, and on warm days they'd been leaving it open, with just a screen. He could go in there.

Would he dare?

Of course he wouldn't, but still, still—

The first time he looked out the vents and saw maple leaves shot through with shades of red and yellow, he panicked. He needed those leaves to hide him on his way to the Sports Family house. If he waited too long, the leaves would be gone.

He began waking up every morning in a cold sweat, thinking, *Maybe today. Do I dare?*

Just thinking about it made his stomach feel funny.

It rained three days in a row in early October, and he was almost relieved because that meant he couldn't go on those days, didn't even have to think about going. He couldn't risk leaving footprints in the mud. And Dad and Matthew and Mark were in the way, hanging around the house and the barn, grumbling because they couldn't get into the fields.

Finally the rain stopped and the fields dried up and Dad and Matthew and Mark went back to their combine and tractors, acres away from the house.

The backyard and the Sports Family's backyard were dry, too.

And it was warm again. The Sports Family left their sliding-glass door open.

The rain hadn't knocked all the leaves off the backyard trees, but the next rain probably would.

On the third morning after the rain, Luke's stomach churned as he sat on his perch watching the neighborhood empty out. He knew without question that today was the day he'd have to go, if he ever intended to. He couldn't wait until spring. He wouldn't be able to stand it.

He watched twenty-eight people leave in eight cars and one school bus. Hands trembling, he made scratches on the wall again and recounted, once, twice, three times. Twenty-eight. Yes. Twenty-eight. Yes. Twenty-eight. The magic number.

He could hear the blood pounding in his ears. He moved in a daze. Off his perch. Down the stairs. Into the kitchen. And then—out the back door.

CHAPTER *THIRTEEN*

He had forgotten what fresh air felt like, filling his nostrils and lungs. It felt good. With his back pressed against the house, he stood still for a moment, just breathing. All the months he'd spent inside suddenly seemed like a dream. He'd been like some confused animal hibernating during nice weather. The last real thing that had happened to him was being called inside when the woods were coming down. Real life was outdoors.

But so was danger. And the longer he stayed out, the greater the danger.

He forced himself down into a crouch and half-crawled, half-ran alongside the house and the hedges and the barn. At the back edge of the barn he hesitated, staring into the seemingly endless gulf between the barn and the trees at the boundary between his backyard and the Sports Family's.

Everybody's gone, he told himself. *There's not a soul around to see you.*

Still, he waited, staring at the blades of grass just beyond his feet. He'd been taught all his life to fear open spaces like the one in front of him. It faced dozens of windows. He'd never stepped foot in any place that public, even if it was deserted.

Still hidden by the barn, he made himself inch his foot forward. Then he drew it back.

He turned around and looked at his family's house, so safe and secure. His sanctuary. He heard his mother's voice in his head: *Luke! Inside. Now.* It seemed so real, he remembered something he'd read in one of the old books in the attic about telepathy—supposedly if people really loved you, they could call out to you from miles away if you were in danger.

He should go back. He'd be safe there.

He took a deep breath, looking forward toward the Sports Family's house, then back again toward his own. He thought about returning home—trudging up the worn stairs, going back to his familiar room and the walls he stared at every day. Suddenly he hated his house. It wasn't a sanctuary. It was a prison.

Before he had time to think again, he pushed himself off into a sprint, recklessly streaking across the grass. He didn't even stop to hide at any trees. He ran right to the Sports Family's door and tugged at the screen.

It was locked.

CHAPTER *FOURTEEN*

In all his plottings, Luke had never thought of the screen door being locked. Though he knew his own parents locked up at night—when they didn't forget—the doors at his house had always been open for him. And he'd never been near anyone else's door.

"Idiot," he muttered to himself.

He tugged harder on the door, but he couldn't concentrate enough to make his hands work together. Each second that passed made the hair on the back of his neck stand up more. He'd never been so exposed in his entire life.

Hurry, hurry, hurry. Get out of sight....

The door didn't budge. He'd have to turn around. Now.

That was what his brain said. What his hand did was plunge through the screen. He pulled the wire away from the frame and reached through. The screen scraped the back of his hand and his arm, but he didn't stop. He fiddled with the lock inside until he heard it click.

He silently slid the screen door back and stepped past the hanging blinds into the Sports Family's house.

Even with the blinds blocking every window, the room he entered was airy and bright. From the freshly painted walls to the sparkling glass tables to the polished wood floor, everything looked new. Luke stared. Almost all the furniture in his own house had been around as long as he could remember, and whatever patterns and designs it originally carried had long ago been worn away. At his house, even the once-orangish couch and the once-greenish chairs were now all a matching sort of brownish gray. This room was different. It reminded him of a word he'd never heard, only read: "pristine." Nobody had ever stepped on these white rugs with manure-covered boots. Nobody had ever sat on those pale blue couches with corn-dust-covered jeans.

Luke might have stood by the door forever, in awe, but someone coughed in another room. Then he heard a strange *be-be-be-beep*. He tiptoed forward. Better to discover than to be discovered.

He went down a long hallway. The beeps had turned into a drawn-out "buzzzzz," coming from a room at the end.

Holding his breath, Luke stopped outside the door to that room and gathered the nerve to peek in. His heart pounded. There was still time to escape unseen, to go back to his house and attic and normal, safe life. But he'd always wonder—

Luke leaned forward slowly, moving a fraction of an inch at a time, until he could just barely see around the door.

Inside the room was a chair and a desk and a big apparatus that Luke vaguely recognized as a computer. And at the computer, typing away furiously, sat a girl.

Luke blinked, thrown off. Somehow he'd never thought about the Sports Family's third child being a girl. She was mostly facing away from Luke, and she wore jeans and a gray sweatshirt not much different from what the Sports Family brothers always wore. Her dark hair was almost as short as Luke's. But there was something about the curve of her cheek, the tilt of her head, the way her sweatshirt clung or didn't cling to her body—all of that made Luke certain she wasn't like him.

He blushed. Then he gulped.

The girl turned her head.

"I—" Luke croaked.

Before he had a chance to think of another word, the girl was across the room and had knocked him down. Then she pinned him to the floor, his arms twisted behind his back, his face buried in the carpet. Luke struggled to turn his head to breathe.

"So," the girl hissed in his ear. "You think you can sneak up on a poor, innocent, unsuspecting girl, who's home all alone? Guess nobody told you about our alarm system. A call went out to our security guards the minute you stepped on our property. They'll be here any second."

Luke panicked. So this was how he'd die. He had to explain. He had to escape.

"No," he said. "They can't come. I—"

"Oh, yeah?" the girl said. "Who are you to stop them?"

Luke raised his head as much as he could. He said the first words that came into his mind.

"Population Police."

The girl let go.

CHAPTER FIFTEEN

Luke sat up, checking his arms to make sure she hadn't broken anything.

"You're lying," the girl said.

But she made no effort to tackle him again. She crouched, looking puzzled for a few moments. Then she grinned.

"I got it! You're another one. Great code word. I'll have to think about using that for the rally."

Now it was Luke's turn to squint in confusion.

The girl giggled.

"I mean, you're another shadow child. Right?"

"Shadow—?" Luke wondered why his brain seemed to be slowing down. Was it just because she seemed several miles ahead of him?

"That's not the term you use?" she asked. "I thought 'shadow child' was universal. But, you know, an illegal, someone whose parents broke Population Law 3903. A third."

"I—" Luke couldn't bring himself to confess. He'd broken so many taboos today, leaving the house, standing in the open yard, talking to a stranger. Why did one more violation matter?

"You can say it," the girl coaxed. " 'I'm a third child.' Why should there be anything wrong with that?"

Luke was spared having to answer her, because she suddenly sprang to her feet, exclaiming, "Oh, no! The alarm!"

She raced down the hall and around the corner. Luke followed to find her jerking open a closet door, then punching buttons on a panel of colored lights.

"Too late. Drat!"

She ran to a phone, Luke following breathlessly. She dialed. Luke watched in amazement. He'd never talked on a phone. His parents had told him the Government could trace calls, could tell if a voice on a phone was from a person who was allowed to exist or not.

"Dad—" She made a face. "I know, I know. Call the security company and get them to cancel the alarm, okay?" Pause. "And might I remind you that the penalty for harboring a shadow child is five million dollars or execution, depending on the mood of the judge?"

She rolled her eyes at Luke while she listened to what seemed to be a long answer.

"Oh, you know. These things happen." Another pause. "Yeah, yeah. Love you, too. Thanks, Dad."

She hung up. Luke wondered if he should run back to his house immediately, before the Population Police really did show up.

"They can find you now," Luke said. "Just from the phone—"

The girl laughed.

"They *say*. But everybody knows the Government's not that competent."

Luke started inching toward the back door, just in case.

"But there really was an alarm?" he asked. "And you have security guards?"

"Sure. Doesn't everyone?" the girl took another look at Luke. "Oh. Maybe not."

She winced apologetically as soon as she'd said that. Luke decided to ignore the insult.

"Do the security guards know you're here?" he asked.

"Of course not," the girl said. "If they came, I'd have to hide. Personally, I think my family just has the alarm system to make sure I stay in the house. They don't know I can disable it. But"—she gave him an evil grin—"I set it off sometimes just for fun."

"That's fun?" Luke asked. He'd thought another third child would understand him, be just like him. This girl sure wasn't. "Aren't you scared the guards might find you?"

"Not really." The girl shrugged. "And see, doing it on purpose every now and then helped us today—my dad didn't really even ask why the system needed to be stopped. He just thought it was me making trouble again."

In a twisted way, she kind of made sense. But trying to figure everything out made Luke's head hurt. He glanced toward the door. If he could just get safely home, he'd never complain about being bored again. Here, he felt as baffled as Alice in Wonderland from one of the old books in the attic. Or—he remembered something he'd read in a nature book—maybe he was like the prey of a snake that hypnotized its victims before it ate them. He didn't think the girl would hurt him, but she might keep him confused and fascinated until the Population Police or the security guards or someone else arrived.

The girl saw where he was looking.

"Am I scaring you?" she asked. "Shadow kids can be so jumpy. You're safe, you know. How about if we start over? Would you care for a seat, uh—what's your name, anyway?"

Luke told her.

"Nice to meet you," the girl said, shaking his hand in a way that made him feel like she was kind of making fun of him. Then she led him to sit down on a couch in the room he'd first entered. She perched beside him. "I'm Jen. Really, it's Jennifer Rose Talbot. But do I look like a Jennifer?"

She shook her head and spread out her arms as if Luke should understand something from her rumpled sweat-shirt and messy hair.

Luke frowned.

"I don't know," he said. "I don't know any Jennifers. Just Matthew and Mark and Mother and Dad." He knew his parents' real names were Edna and Harlan, but he wondered if he shouldn't keep that secret. Just in case. Probably he shouldn't have even mentioned Matthew and

Mark, but he was surprised into it, thinking suddenly about how there was a world full of people outside his house, with a world full of different names he'd never heard of.

"Hmm," the girl said. "Then I have to explain—a Jennifer's supposed to be, like, really girly and prissy. So the joke's on Mom. She wanted some frilly little girl she could put in lacy dresses and sit in the corner. Like a doll." She paused. "Are Matthew and Mark your older brothers?"

Luke nodded.

"So you've never met anyone outside your immediate family?"

Luke shook his head no. Jen looked so amazed, he felt he had to defend himself.

"And you have?" he asked, with almost the same taunting voice he sometimes used with Mark.

"Well, yeah," she said.

"But you're a third child, too," Luke protested. "A shadow child. Right?"

He suddenly felt like it might be easy to cry, if he let himself. All his life, he'd been told he couldn't do everything Matthew and Mark did because he was the third child. But if Jen could go about freely, it didn't make sense. Had his parents lied?

"Don't you have to hide?" he asked.

"Sure," Jen said. "Mostly. But my parents are very good at bribery. And so am I." She grinned wickedly. Then she squinted at Luke. "How *did* you know I was a third child? How did you know I was here?"

Luke told her. Somehow it seemed important to start with the woods coming down, so it turned into a very long story. Jen interrupted frequently with questions and comments—"So you've never been away from your house except to go to your backyard or barn?"; "You've stayed inside for six months?"; and "Gosh, you must really hate these houses, huh?" And then, when he got to the part about seeing her face in the window, she bit her lip.

"My dad would kill me if he knew I'd done that. But the mirrors were messed up, and Carlos bet me I didn't even know what the weather was outside, and—"

"Huh?" Luke said. "Mirrors? Carlos?"

Jen waved away his questions.

"Luke Garner," she announced solemnly, "you have come to the right place. Forget that hiding-like-a-mole stuff. I'm your ticket out."

CHAPTER SIXTEEN

Want any more potatoes, Luke?" Mother offered that night at supper. "Luke?" Her voice got more insistent. "LUKE?"

Luke jerked his attention back to his family. Mother was holding the bowl of mashed potatoes out to him.

"Er—no," Luke said. "No thanks. I've still got some."

"More for me!" Mark crowed.

Luke tuned them out again. He'd barely eaten his first serving of potatoes, he'd been so busy thinking about his secret visit to the Sports Family house. He couldn't believe he'd dared to go. Just the thought of his run through their yard made his heart beat fast, remembering fear and pride. He'd really done it.

And then meeting Jen was—amazing. There was no other word for it. He was so overwhelmed with wonder at everything he'd seen at her house, everything she'd told him, that he started to say, "Did you know that Jen—"

At the last minute, he clamped his teeth shut, holding the words in. He thought he'd burst. He could feel his face flush red with the effort of keeping still. He bent his head low over his plate so nobody would see. How could he ever manage to keep Jen secret? But he had to, because if he told, they'd forbid him to go back.

And he had to go back.

"We'll set up a signal," Jen had said. "Something I can see—"

"But you don't have vents to look out like I do," Luke protested. "You can't look out the windows."

"Oh, when the mirrors work, it's not a problem. Look." She took him over to a window near the sliding-glass door and showed him a mirror that reflected a wide view of the Talbots' backyard and the landscape beyond. It showed just the corner of the Garners' barn, but when Jen turned it a bit, the entire Garner house came into view. Luke wondered if his parents could set up the same kind of system. Then he looked at the mirror again and decided it might be expensive. And, anyway, how would he explain where he'd gotten the idea?

"So, let's see," Jen said. "A signal. I've got it—how about if I look out every morning at nine, and if you can come over, you shine a flashlight at me. I'll shine one back if everything's safe."

"We don't have any flashlights," Luke said. "Not that work, I mean."

Jen frowned.

"Why not?"

"We haven't had any batteries in, I don't know, four or five years," Luke explained. In fact, he felt proud even to remember what a flashlight was.

"Okay, okay," Jen said. "No flashlight, no computer—"

"Oh, we have a computer," Luke said. "My parents do. And I think it still works. But it's in Dad's office in the front of the house, and I'm not allowed in there. And, anyhow, I'd never be allowed to touch the computer." He remembered once when he was very young, maybe three or four, and he'd followed Mother into Dad's office while she was cleaning. The rows of letters on the computer keyboard had looked like a toy to him, and he'd reached one finger up and tapped the space bar, over and over again. Mother had turned around and freaked out.

"They can find you now!" she'd screamed. "If they were watching—"

And for weeks after that, she'd hidden him even more carefully than ever, locking him in his room when she had to go outside.

Jen rolled her eyes.

"Don't tell me your family believes that Government propaganda stuff," she said. "They've spent so much money trying to convince people they can monitor all the TVs and computers, you know they couldn't have afforded to actually do it. I've been using our computer since I was three—and watching TV, too—and they've never caught me. How about a candle?"

"What?" It took Luke a minute to realize she was talking about the signal again. "The candles—they're all in the kitchen, and I'm not allowed—"

Jen mimicked the words as he said them: "—to go in there."

"They've got you on an awfully short leash, don't they?" she asked.

"No. I mean, yes. But they're just trying to protect me—"

Jen shook her head. "Yeah, I've heard that one. Ever hear of disobeying?"

"I—" Luke started defensively. "I'm here, aren't I?"

Jen laughed. "Got me. But, listen, if you can't do candles or a flashlight, how about just turning on a light that I can see?"

Luke was quicker this time figuring out that she was still talking about the signal.

"The one by the back door," Luke said. "You can't miss it."

He wasn't allowed to turn that on, either, but he didn't dare say "not allowed" again.

Now Luke toyed with his mashed potatoes. His entire conversation with Jen had been like that—she mocked, he defended, but she always got her way.

Of course—he defended her to himself—she knew and had seen so much more than him. After he'd finished his story on the couch, she'd told him hers.

"First," she'd said defiantly, "my parents had me on purpose. Thirteen years ago. Mom already had Bull and Brawn from her first marriage—"

"Your brothers?" Luke asked.

"Yeah. Buellton and Brownley, really, but what kind of names are those for knuckleheads like them? Mom was going through some snobbish upper-class phase with husband number one."

"She's had more than one husband?" Luke asked. He didn't know that was possible.

"Sure," Jen said. "Dad—who's really my stepdad—is number three."

Luke found that so confusing, he just kept his mouth shut.

"Anyhow," Jen said. "Mom was dying to have a little girl, so when she and husband number two got together, she went and paid some doctor lots of money so she could get pregnant."

"What if you'd been a boy?" Luke asked.

"Oh, they got in on the beginning of the gender selection experiments." Luke must have given Jen a particularly blank look, because she explained it. "That means they made sure I was a girl. Doctors can do that, you know, but the Government outlawed the procedure because they were afraid it'd throw the population even more out of whack. I'm sure my parents paid a lot for it. Were your mom and dad trying for a girl?"

Luke thought about it. He remembered Mother saying she'd wanted four boys, but would she have wanted a girl even more? Someone like Mother? He couldn't really picture a girl in his house.

"They weren't trying for anything," he said. "I was a surprise. Luck."

Jen nodded. "I didn't think they paid for you," she said. Then she put her hand over her mouth. "That sounded really terrible, didn't it? I didn't mean anything by it. It's just—you're the first person I've met who wasn't a Baron."

"How do you know I'm not?" Luke asked stiffly.

"Well—" Jen waved her hand in a way that made Luke even more aware of the contrast between his ragged flannel shirt and patched jeans, and Jen's perfect house. "Look, don't be mad. It doesn't matter. Or maybe it does, but I think it's cool that you're not a Baron. You can help me even more."

"Help?" Luke asked.

"With the rally," Jen said. She bit her lip. "Should I— there's no way you could be an infiltrator, is there? Can I trust you?"

"Of course you can," Luke said. He felt insulted again.

Jen leaned her head back and stared at the ceiling, as if an answer were written there. Then she looked back at Luke.

"I'm sorry. I'm botching this. I'm not used to really talking, just on the Net. Look, I trust you, but I'm not the only one involved. So let's wait, okay?"

"Okay," Luke said. But he couldn't help sounding injured.

Jen leaned over and gave his shoulders a quick shake.

"Oh, don't say it like that. Say, 'Okay, Jen, I respect your judgment.' Or, 'Okay, Jen, whatever you think is best.'" She giggled. "That's what Dad tells me I should say when I disagree with him. Can you believe it? Lawyers!"

Luke was glad the subject had changed. "Your dad's a lawyer?" he asked.

Jen rolled her eyes. "Yeah, all Mom's husbands have been. Strange taste, huh? Number one was an environmental lawyer, of all things; number two was corporate—that's how they had enough money to get me. And number three, Dad, is with the Government. High up, I might add."

"But—if you're an illegal—" Luke hadn't thought he could get any more confused.

Jen laughed.

"Haven't you learned? Government leaders are the worst ones for breaking laws. How do you think we got this house? How do you think I got Internet access? How do you think we live?"

"I don't know," Luke said, fully honest. "I don't think I know much of anything."

Jen patted his head, as if he were a little kid or a dog.

"That's okay," she said. "You'll learn."

It wasn't long after that that Luke said he had to leave, because he was afraid Dad or Matthew or Mark might come in for lunch a little early. He dreaded the trip back. Jen walked him to the door, chattering the whole way.

"I'll fix the screen and deal with the security system, so

no one will ever know you were here," she said. "And—oh, no!"

Luke followed her gaze. She was staring at three pin-points of blood on the carpet.

"I'm sorry," Luke said. "That must be from when I scraped my hand. I'll clean it up. There's still time—"

Secretly, he was glad of the delay.

"No, no," Jen said impatiently. "I don't care about the carpet. It's just that Mom and Dad will know, and when they see I don't have any cuts—"

And then, before Luke even knew what she was doing, she thrust her hand toward the torn part of the screen. The jagged edge didn't cut immediately, so she held the screen with her right hand and raked it across her left. When Jen pulled her hand back, Luke saw a gash even deeper than his. Jen squeezed out a few drops of blood and let them fall to the carpet.

"There," she said.

Stunned, Luke backed out the door.

"Come back soon, farmer boy," Jen said.

Luke turned and ran, blindly, not even slowing down to creep alongside the barn. He went straight to the back door of his house, yanked it open, and let it bang shut behind him.

Now, sitting at supper, he felt his heart pounding again as he thought of how dangerous that had been. Why hadn't he looked first? Why hadn't he crawled? He poked his fork into his potatoes, now gone cold and congealed. He watched Mother gathering up dirty dishes while Dad, Matthew, and Mark leaned back in their chairs, talking of grain yields. Jen had scared him—that was why. Seeing her cut her hand had terrified him. How could she do something like that for him, when they'd just met?

CHAPTER *SEVENTEEN*

Luke spent practically every second of the next three days either reliving his secret visit to Jen or planning another one. The first day, a Government inspector came out to examine the Garners' crop, so Luke stayed in his room the entire day. The second day it rained, and Dad spent the morning doing book work in the house. The third day, Dad was back in the fields, but when Luke crept over to the back door promptly at 9 A.M. and daringly flipped the light switch, he got no answering flash from Jen's house. Maybe the clocks in her house were slow. He left the light on for fifteen whole minutes, terrified the whole time that someone besides Jen might see it. Finally, heartsick, he switched it off and climbed with shaky legs back to his room.

What if something had happened to Jen? What if she were sick—dying, even—alone in her house? What if she'd been caught or turned in? Just from the little time Luke had spent with her, he could tell: She took a lot of risks.

It never had occurred to him that knowing another

person would give him someone else to worry about.

He steadied himself by leaning against the wall at the top of the stairs and reminded himself of less frightening possibilities: Maybe one of her parents was just out running errands, not working, so they were going to be home soon. Maybe…he tried to think of another safe reason Jen hadn't signaled for him to come. But he had so much trouble picturing her ordinary life that his imagination failed him.

He found out the next day, when he risked a dash to Jen's house as soon as Jen answered his signal.

"Where were you?" he asked instantly.

"When? Yesterday?" She yawned, sliding the door shut behind him. "Did you try to come over? I'm sorry. Mom had a free day and made me go shopping."

Luke gaped at her. "Shopping? You went out?"

Jen nodded nonchalantly.

"But I didn't see you leave—" Luke protested.

Jen looked at him as if she seriously wondered if he had a brain. "Of course not. I was hiding. The backseat of our car is hollowed out—Dad had it custom-built."

"You went out—" Luke repeated in awe.

"Well, it's not like I saw anything until we got to the mall. Two hours of riding in the dark is not my idea of fun. I hate it."

"But at the mall—you got out? You didn't have to hide?"

Jen laughed at his amazement.

"Mom got me a forged shopping pass a long time ago.

Supposedly, I'm her niece. It's good enough to convince store clerks, but if the Population Police ever found me in a roadside stop, I'd be dead. There you have it, my mother's priorities. Shopping is more important than my life."

Luke shook his head and sat down on the couch because his knees were feeling a little shaky.

"I didn't know," he said. "I didn't know thirds could do that."

What if Mother and Dad got him a forged pass? For a minute he could almost picture it—they could hide him under burlap bags in the pickup truck bed until they got into town.

Everybody in town knew Mother and Dad. Everybody knew Mother and Dad had only two sons. Matthew and Mark.

"You went to the city," he said.

"Well, yeah," Jen said. "You don't see any malls around here, do you?"

"What was it like?" Luke almost whispered.

"Boring," Jen said. "Really, really boring. Mom wanted to buy me a dress—who knows why—so we went to one store after another, and I had to try on all these dresses that scratched and pricked and poked me. And then she made me get a bunch of bras—oh, sorry," she said when Luke blushed a deep red. "I guess you don't talk much about bras at your house."

"Matthew and Mark do, sometimes, when they're being...dirty," Luke said.

"Well, bras aren't *dirty*," Jen said. "They're just torture devices invented by men or mothers or something."

"Oh," Luke said, looking down.

"But, anyway," Jen said, with a bounce that propelled her off the couch. "I checked you out on the computer and you're all right, you don't exist. Not officially, anyway. So you're safe. And—"

Hearing Jen say that so flippantly—*you don't exist*—made Luke feel funny.

"How do you know I'm safe?" he interrupted.

"Fingerprints," Jen said. When Luke gave her a blank look, she explained. "My brother Brawn went through this phase where he wanted to be a detective—not that he ever would have been smart enough for it—and I remembered he still has a fingerprinting kit. So I dusted for your fingerprints on things you touched, just like on TV. I got a really good print off the wall. Then I scanned that into the computer, linked into the national file of fingerprints and, *voilà*, I discovered your fingerprints don't exist, so neither do you. Officially."

She made a mocking face for emphasis. Luke wanted to ask, *The Population Police can't find me because of what you did, can they?* But he understood so little of what she'd explained that he didn't think it would help to ask anything. And Jen was already onto the next thought.

"And, anyhow, you seem trustworthy. So-oo, now that I know you're safe, I can tell you about the rally and show you our secret chat rooms and everything—"

Jen was already leaving the room, so he had to follow just to hear the rest of her sentence.

"Want something to eat or drink?" she asked, hesitating at the doorway to the grand kitchen. "I was so surprised, I forgot to be a good hostess the last time. What'll it be? Soda? Potato chips?"

"But those are illegal," Luke protested. He remembered reading something about junk food in one of the books in the attic and asking his mother about it. She'd explained that it was something people used to eat all the time, until the Government shut down the factories that made it. She wouldn't tell him why. But, as a special treat, she'd brought out a bag of potato chips she'd been saving for years and shared them, just with him. They were salty, but hard to chew. Luke had pretended to like them only because Mother seemed to want him to.

"Yeah, well, we're illegal, too, so why shouldn't we enjoy ourselves?" Jen asked, thrusting a bowl of chips at him. To be polite, Luke took one chip. And then another. And another. These potato chips were so good, he had to hold himself back from grabbing them by the handful. Jen stared at him.

"Do you go hungry sometimes?" she asked in a low voice.

"No," Luke said in surprise.

"Some shadow children do because they don't have food ration cards, and the rest of their family doesn't share," she said, opening a refrigerator that was bigger than every appliance in the Garners' kitchen put together. "My family can get all the food we want, of course, but"—she looked at him in a way that once again made him conscious of his ragged clothes—"How does your family get food for you?"

The question puzzled Luke.

"The same way they get it for themselves," he said. "We grow it. We have a garden—I used to work in it a lot, before, you know. And then, we have the hogs, or used to, and I guess sometimes we'd trade a butchered hog for someone else's butchered steer, so we'd have beef—"

Those were all shadowy transactions in Luke's mind. He had to strain his brain to remember overhearing Dad or Matthew reporting to Mother, "Ready to cook some steak? Johnston up near Libertyville wants some ham..."

Jen dropped a plastic bottle full of brown liquid. "You eat *meat*?" she exclaimed.

"Sure. Don't you?" Luke asked.

"When Dad can get it," Jen said, bending to pick up the bottle. She poured a glassful for Luke and one for herself. Both drinks fizzed and bubbled. "Even his clout isn't *that* great. The Government's been trying to force everyone, even the Barons, to become vegetarians."

"Why?" Luke asked.

Jen handed him his glass.

"Something about vegetables being more efficient," she said. "Farmers have to use a lot more land to produce one pound of meat than to produce a pound of—what's it called?—soybeans."

Luke wrinkled his nose at the thought of eating soybeans.

"I don't know," he said slowly. "We always fed our hogs the grain we couldn't sell because it didn't meet Government standards. But since the Government made us get rid of our hogs, Dad just lets that grain rot in the field."

"Really?" Jen grinned as if he'd just announced the overthrow of the Government. She thumped him on the back just as he took his first sip of soda. Between the bubbly drink and her enthusiastic pounding, Luke started coughing. Jen didn't seem to notice. "See, I told you you'd be a big help. I'm going to go post that on a bulletin board right now!"

"Wait—" Luke sputtered between coughs. He didn't know what she was talking about. But he couldn't let her get his family in trouble. He chased her down the hall, catching up just as she was sliding into the chair in front of the computer. She switched it on, and it made the *be-be-be-be-beeep* sounds Luke had heard the last time. Luke stood to the side, carefully out of sight of the screen.

"It's not going to bite you," Jen said. "Grab a chair. Sit down."

Luke inched back.

"But the Government—" he said.

"The Government's incompetent and stupid," Jen said. "Get it? Believe me, if they were watching through my computer screen, I'd know by now."

Meekly, Luke pulled over a padded chair and sat down.

He watched as Jen typed in, "If the Government let farmers feed their animals the grain they can't sell, there'd be more meat."

Luke was relieved that she hadn't mentioned his family. But, unless the Government was spying on them, he couldn't understand what difference it made for her to write that.

"Where'd that go?" he asked as the words disappeared. "Who's going to see it?"

"I put it on a Department of Agriculture bulletin board. Anyone with a computer can find it now. Maybe a Government worker with half a brain will see it and actually think for the first time this decade."

"But—" Luke squinted in confusion. "Why does it matter?"

Jen fixed her gaze on Luke.

"You don't even know, do you?" she asked. "You don't know why they passed the Population Law."

"N-no," Luke admitted.

"It's all about food," Jen said. "The Government was scared we'd all run out of food if the population kept growing. That's why they made you and me illegal, to keep people from starving."

Luke suddenly felt doubly guilty for the potato chips he was still cramming into his mouth. He swallowed hard and lowered his hands to his lap, instead of back into the chip bowl.

"So if I didn't eat, my food would go to someone who

was legal," Luke said. But in his family, that would just be Matthew or Mark, and they were hardly starving. Matthew was even starting to sport the same roll of fat around his waist that Dad had. Then Luke remembered the tramp from long ago, saying, "I ain't et in three days...." Was that Luke's fault?

Jen laughed.

"Stop looking so worried," she said. "That *is* what the Government thinks, but they're wrong. My dad says there's plenty of food, it's just not distributed right. That's why they've got to stop the Population Law. That's why they've got to recognize you and me and all the other shadow kids. That's why we're going to have the rally."

As ignorant as he was, Luke could tell from the way she said it that the rally was important.

"Can you tell me about the rally now?" he asked humbly.

"Yes," Jen said. She pushed away from the computer and twirled on her chair. "Hundreds of us—all the shadow children I could track down—are going to march on the Government in protest. We'll go right to the president's house. We won't leave them alone until they give us the same rights everybody else has."

Just my luck, Luke thought. I finally meet another third child, and she's absolutely crazy.

"And"—Jen said, as bubbly as the shaken soda—"You can come, too. Won't it be great?"

CHAPTER *EIGHTEEN*

—" Luke said. He couldn't look at Jen's triumphant grin. "I don't think I—"

He thought about how terrifying it was just running back and forth between his house and Jen's. Even this morning, on his third run through their yards, his heart had pounded so hard, he'd wondered if it could burst from fear. And in the yard at least, he was sure—or as sure as he could be—that no one was watching. How could Jen think he would dare go out in public, where he knew people could see him—people in Government, no less—and say, "I am a third child! I want to be treated like everyone else!"

"Scared?" Jen said softly.

Luke could only nod.

Jen turned back to the computer.

"Well, I am, too," she said matter-of-factly. She typed something, then looked back at Luke. "Some. But don't you think it'll be a relief? No more hiding, no more pretending, just—being free!"

Luke wondered if he'd always misunderstood the meaning of the word "relief." Jen's rally sounded like his worst nightmare.

"You can think about it," she said. "You don't have to decide anything today. Now, ready to chat?"

Luke looked back at the computer screen, where rows of words were unfurling:

Carlos: It's 105 here, and my parents think it's a waste to run the a.c. during the day. Can you say heartless?

Sean: Why don't you just crank it up, then turn it off again right before they get home? That's what Pat and I do. They'll never know.

Carlos: Yeah, but my parents probably read their electric bill.

Yolanda: So what are they going to do? Ground you?

Carlos: Good point. I'm searching for the temp control right now.

Yolanda: Where's Jen?

Sean: You know she never gets up this early.

Carlos: Curses—my parents have the temp control locked somehow. Told you they were evil. Where is Jen? I can't wait for her sarcarstic comment.

Luke read the words Jen was typing: "I'm right here, and, Sean, I do so get up early. I just don't always choose to see *you* first thing. And Carlos—what's wrong? Is there sweat in your eyes? There's only one 'r' in 'sarcastic.'"

She hit another key, and the words appeared right up

with everyone else's. They were followed quickly by another line:

Sean: Good morning to you, too, Jen. Glad to see you're still among the living.

Jen typed quickly: "No, just among the hidden. Not the same thing at all!!!!" Then she sent it, too.

"What is this?" Luke asked. "Some sort of game?"

He remembered Jen mentioning a Carlos before, and never explaining who he was. Were these some sort of computerized imaginary friends?

"Carlos, Sean, Yolanda—they're all other third children. Sean's even got a brother, Pat, who's a fourth child. This is how I talk to them."

Luke watched the next line of type appear: "Carlos: Thanks for the sympathy, Jen."

"But how—?" Luke asked, still doubtful.

"Oh, you know. It's the Net," Jen said. "If you've got a spare hour or two sometime, I'll give you the technical gobbledygook to explain it. All I care about is that it works. I'd die without someone to talk to."

She was typing even as she talked. Luke craned his head to see what she wrote: "Guess what? The kid I told you about, Luke, is here with me."

Quickly, three "Hi, Luke"s appeared on the screen.

Luke fought down panic.

"But the Government—" he said. "They'll find me—"

Jen playfully slugged his arm. "Chill, okay? Nobody from the Government can get in this chat room. We all use a password. Just third children know it. And, anyhow, even if someone else read this, what would they know? Just that somewhere in the world, there's a kid named Luke. Big deal."

"But they can trace you through the computer, and then they'd find me, too." Luke's heart was still pounding.

"Look, if they could trace people through the computer, or through this chat room, wouldn't they have found me a long time ago?" Jen asked.

Luke tried to think clearly. "Your parents," he said. "You said they bribe people. So you're safe. But mine—"

Jen was shaking her head.

"No, I'm not safe," she said grimly. "Even my parents couldn't bribe the Population Police if they found me. Maybe to keep them from looking—but maybe not even that. The Population Police get some ridiculously big reward for every illegal they find. Why do you think I hide at all? Why do you think we have to have the rally? *Everybody* ought to be safe. And nobody should have to use bribes just to walk down the street or go to a mall or take a ride in a car...."

Luke glanced back at the computer screen, where the conversation continued.

"How did all those people find out the password?" he asked. "How did you?"

"Well, I created the chat room, so I made it up," Jen said.

"And I knew a couple other shadow kids, and I got my parents and their parents to get the password to them. And then some of those kids spread the password to other kids they knew. Last time I counted, I had contact with eight hundred kids."

Luke shook his head. He didn't think even his parents knew that many people.

"So what is the password?" he asked.

" 'Free,' " Jen said. "It's 'free.' "

CHAPTER *NINETEEN*

Luke left Jen's that day with a pile of books and computer printouts clutched to his chest.

"Some reading material for you," she'd said. "So you'll understand."

Back in his own room, Luke sat down on his bed and opened the first book. It was thick and carried its title in ominous black letters: THE POPULATION DISASTER. The type inside was small and closely spaced. Luke read a sentence at random: "While debate continues over the carrying capacity of the earth—" He skipped ahead. "If the Total Fertility Rate in industrialized countries had remained at or below 2.1—" Luke saw that reading this book would be like puzzling out the letters Dad got from the Government. He glanced at the other two books: *The Famine Years Revisited* and *The Population Reversal*. They looked no easier. The computer printouts were at least brief, but both "The Problem of the Shadows" and "The Population Law: Our Country's Biggest Mistake," were full of big words.

Luke sighed. He was tempted to put the books aside and just ask Jen to explain them to him. And he might have, except for what she'd said as she'd begun handing them to him. "Oh, my gosh! I didn't think—you can read, can't you?"

"Of course," Luke had answered stiffly. "I was reading in the chat room, wasn't I?"

"Yes, but you could have been—oh, never mind. I've offended you again, haven't I? Me and my big mouth. It wouldn't have been anything to be ashamed of, even if you couldn't. Oh, I'm making things worse. I'll shut up. Here."

And it had seemed to Luke that she'd pulled even bigger books off the bookshelves after that.

Now he resolutely turned to the beginning of *The Population Disaster* and began reading: "Since some elements of the overpopulation crisis were foreseen in the 1800s, an uninformed observer could only wonder why humankind came so near to total annihilation. But—"

Luke reached for the dictionary and settled in for the long haul.

It rained for the next several days, so Luke read constantly, not even tempted to race over to Jen's instead. He could hear Dad banging around downstairs, stomping in and out from the barn or the machine shed. Now that the harvest was in, Luke thought Dad might be bored without the pigs to take care of. So Luke read cautiously, always ready to shove his population book under his pillow and replace it with one of his adventure books. The preparation paid off on the fourth day, when he heard Dad's footsteps on the stairs.

"Hey, Luke, what're you up to?"

"Nothing," Luke said, turning *Treasure Island* right side up at the very last moment. Dad didn't notice.

"Want to play cards?"

They played rummy on Luke's bed. Luke could feel the corner of *The Population Disaster* poking his back throughout the entire game. And he kept wanting to ask Dad about what he was learning. He spent most of the first game biting his tongue. Dad won.

"Again?" Dad asked, shuffling the cards.

"If you don't have any work you've got to do."

"In November? With no livestock? Only work I've got now is figuring out how we're going to pay our bills once the hog money runs out."

"Isn't there some way to grow stuff inside during the winter? Like down in the basement, with special lights, lots of water and extra minerals. And then you could sell it?" Luke asked without thinking. He'd just finished reading a chapter in the population book about hydroponics.

Dad squinted.

"Seems I did hear tell of that once."

Luke won the next hand. Dad didn't seem to be concentrating. At the end, Dad said, "Mind if we quit now?"

Luke was terrified Dad would ask where he'd heard of hydroponics. So he just said, "No problem."

Dad left muttering, "Growing food inside...hmmm..."

Luke wished he'd had the nerve to ask about the Population Law, or the famines, or even some family history.

Once he got past the dense language, the books Jen had loaned him were full of revelations. As best he could understand it, the world had simply gotten too full of people about twenty years earlier. Poor countries had it particularly bad, and people there often starved or were malnourished. But then something worse happened: Terrible droughts struck the parts of the world that always grew the most food. For three years, they grew almost nothing. People everywhere starved. In Luke's country, the Government began rationing food, only allowing people to have 1,500 calories a day. And, to make sure there was food, they seized control of all food production. They forced factories that had made junk food to crank out healthy food instead. They forced farmers to move to land that would be more likely to produce. *(Is that why we don't live near our grandparents?* Luke wanted to ask his parents.) But the Government didn't think that was enough. They wanted to make sure there would never again be more people than the farmers could feed. So they passed the Population Law, too.

In the evenings, spooning in his stew or cutting up his meat, Luke felt pangs of guilt now. Perhaps someone was starving someplace because of him. But the food wasn't *there*—wherever the starving people were—it was *here*, on his plate. He ate it all.

"Luke, you're so quiet lately. Is everything all right?" Mother asked one night when he waved away second helpings of cabbage.

"I'm fine," he said, and went back to eating silently.

But he was worrying. Worrying that maybe the Government was right and that he shouldn't exist.

Only when he got to the two computer printouts did he begin to feel better. One of the articles began, "The Population Law is evil." The other said, "Hundreds of children are hidden, mistreated, starved, neglected, abused—even murdered—for no reason. Forcing children into the shadows can be counted as genocide."

"How can this be?" he asked Jen a week later when he finally got a chance to go back to her house. "How can the books and the articles be so different?"

She handed him a glass of soda.

"What do you mean?" she asked.

Luke pointed to *The Population Disaster*. "This book says the human race would have gone extinct if we hadn't had the Population Law. And this"—he held up and shook "The Problem of the Shadows" article—"this says the Population Law was totally unnecessary and cruel. It says there was plenty of food, even during the famines, except that the Barons were hoarding it." Belatedly, he remembered that Jen was a Baron. "Sorry."

Jen shrugged, not the least bit offended.

"So what's the truth?" Luke asked.

Jen shook potato chips into a bowl.

"Well, think about it. The Government allowed those books to be published—they probably even paid for them. So of course they're going to say what the Government wants people to believe. They're just propaganda. Lies. But the articles, the authors of those probably put themselves at risk getting the information out. So they're right."

Luke pondered that. "Then why'd you make me read the books?" he asked.

"So you'd understand how stupid the Government is," Jen said. "So you'd understand why we have to make them see the truth."

Luke looked at the stack of thick books on the Talbots' kitchen counter. They looked so official, so important—who was he to say they weren't true?

CHAPTER *TWENTY*

Luke feared he'd have to wait months between visits to Jen once the snow started. But the weather proved kind that winter—most days were dry and clear. He didn't have leafy trees to hide behind, but he began to feel safe, anyway, crawling through his and Jen's backyards. By mid-January he could make the entire journey without his heart beating abnormally at all. The odds against someone watching from one of the other Baron houses seemed too astronomical to worry about. His only concern was Dad.

Dad usually hung around the house a lot during the winter. Without the hogs to tend to, he could easily have been there even more than usual, preventing Luke from ever sneaking out. But suddenly Dad had taken to heading to town many mornings, yelling up to Luke, "I'm going to the library. You've got something up there to eat for lunch, don't you?" or, "There's some plastic tubing over to Slyton I want to check out. Tell the boys when they get in from school, you hear?"

"It's that hydroponics notion," Luke bragged to Jen one day in late January while they were sitting at the computer together. "I got Dad all excited about it, and now he's too busy with that to notice what I do."

"What's hydroponics?" Jen asked.

"It was in one of your books—you know, growing plants indoors, without soil, just using water and special minerals."

"Oh," Jen said. "Does he think the Government would actually let him do that?"

"I guess so," Luke said. "Why wouldn't they?"

Jen shrugged. "Why does the Government do anything?"

Luke didn't have an answer to that. Jen turned back to the computer chat room, where everyone was debating fake I.D.'s.

Carlos: Mom says they won't buy me one until I'm 18, because she thinks the Gov. wouldn't challenge an adult's as much. And maybe they'll be cheaper then.

Pat: Maybe Sean and I will get ours by the time we're ninety. Dad and Mom have been saving for them as long as we can remember.

Yolanda: My dad sez he's waiting to find one that's foolproof. He sez there are too many bad ones out there.

Jen began typing furiously. "Who needs a fake I.D.? Carlos, they'd probably get one for you that says 'John Smith,' and you'd have to spend the rest of your life trying to pass for an Anglo. My parents have been begging me to get a fake I.D. for years, but I won't until I can have one that says 'Jen Talbot' and is really *mine*.

"Have you all forgotten the rally? We're all gonna get real I.D.'s that say who we really are!!!! WE AREN'T FAKES! WE SHOULDN'T HAVE TO HIDE!"

She jabbed the Enter button so hard, the computer shook.

"But, Jen," Luke said timidly, "I thought you used a fake I.D. to go shopping with your mom. It said you were her niece."

Jen turned her fierce gaze to Luke.

"No, that was just a shopping pass," she said. "I don't like using that, either, but I figured I can't fight my parents about everything. What they're talking about"—she pointed at the computer screen—"is taking on a fake identity permanently. Most shadow kids do that eventually—they go live with another family and pretend to be someone they aren't for the rest of their lives."

"So you'd rather hide?" Luke asked. He thought about using a different name, living in a different family, being a different person. He couldn't imagine it.

"No, of course I wouldn't rather hide," Jen said irritably. "But getting one of those I.D.'s—that's just a different way of hiding. I want to be me and go about like anybody else. There's no compromise. Which is why I've got to convince these idiots that the rally's their only chance."

There was a shocked blankness on the computer screen after Jen's entry. Then Carlos ventured, "Um, Jen, got any of your parents' blood pressure medicine handy? Sounds like you need it."

Jen stabbed the power button on the computer. The screen instantly went dark. She spun around in her chair and clenched her fists.

"Argh!" she screamed, with a grimace of frustration.

"Jen?" Luke asked. He leaned away from her in case she decided to use those clenched fists.

Jen turned to Luke in surprise, as though she'd forgotten he was there.

"Don't you ever feel like saying, 'I can't take this anymore'?" she asked. She leaped up and began pacing the floor. "Don't you ever want to just walk out into the sunshine and say, 'Forget hiding! I don't care!'? Am I the only one who feels this way?"

"No," Luke whispered.

She whirled around and pointed at the computer.

"Then what's wrong with them? Why don't they understand? Why aren't they taking this seriously?"

Luke bit his lip.

"I think," he said, "people just have different ways of expressing what they feel. Those kids make jokes and complain. You run around screaming your head off and tackling people."

He was proud of himself for figuring that out, considering he really only knew five people in the whole world. But for the first time, he wondered how the rest of his family would cope if any of them had to hide. Dad would get grumpy. Mother would try to make the best of it, but you'd be able to tell that she was really unhappy. Matthew would be quiet, but would look sad all the time, the way he looked every time anyone mentioned the pigs they couldn't keep anymore. Mark would gripe so much that he'd make everyone miserable. For the first time, Luke felt a glimmer of pride, that he dealt with hiding better than anyone else in his family would. He thought.

Jen snorted at his explanation. "Whatever," she said. She slid back into her chair by the computer. "But the rally's in April. I've got three months to make sure everyone's ready."

She switched on the computer and began typing furiously again.

Luke slipped away a few hours later. He wasn't sure Jen noticed him leaving.

CHAPTER *TWENTY-ONE*

I n February, Dad got the letter from the Government forbidding him from trying to grow anything indoors.

"It has come to our attention that you have been purchasing excess amounts of plastic pipe, such as is used in the germination, cultivation, and development of vegetative matter in an interior structure," the letter began. "Due to the preponderance of such agricultural methods in the cultivation of illegal substances, we order you to cease and desist immediately...."

Luke read the letter at supper, after everyone else in the family had had a stab at trying to figure out what it meant. Somehow, after reading all the big books that Jen had loaned him, he didn't find the fancy words so daunting.

"They want you to stop," Luke said. "They're scared you're going to grow something illegal. And this part"— he pointed at the letter, although everyone else was at the table, several feet away, and he was in his usual spot on the stairs—"this part, where they say, 'render all such materials for our adjudication,' that means you have to turn over all the stuff you bought and they'll decide if they're going to fine you or not."

The rest of the family looked at Luke in amazement. Then Mark started giggling.

"Drugs," he said. "They think you're going to grow drugs."

Dad flashed him a look of pure disgust.

"Think it's funny? We'll see what you think next year when your feet grow and we don't have money for new shoes."

Mark stopped laughing.

"We'll get by," Luke's mother said quietly. "We always have."

Dad shoved back from the table.

"Why didn't I get a permit?" he asked no one in particular. "Maybe if I just get a permit—"

By then, Luke had read the rest of the letter.

"They don't give out permits for hydroponics," he said. "This says it's always illegal."

This time he only got a glare from Dad.

Luke felt his father's disappointment, and seeing his parents so worried about money made a small voice whisper in the back of his head, *Maybe if they didn't have you, they could afford everything they want.* But he didn't eat that much, and all of his clothes were hand-me-downs from Matthew and Mark. And how much could it cost to heat his attic room? Sometimes he found ice crystals on the chair he sat in to watch the neighborhood. He tried to ignore the voice.

What bothered him more was that, without the hydro-ponics idea to keep him busy, Dad barely left the farm for the rest of the winter. Luke made it over to Jen's only once in all of February, and twice in March, when Dad began driving around looking for the best seed corn prices.

But each time, Jen greeted him with big hugs and acted genuinely thrilled to see him. Her tantrum in January seemed forgotten. One day, the two of them made a huge mess of the Talbots' kitchen baking cookies.

"Won't your parents mind?" Luke asked when Jen scolded him for attempting to clean the flour handprints off the cabinets and refrigerator and stove.

"Are you kidding? I want this preserved. They'll be thrilled to see any sign of domesticity on my part," Jen said.

Another time, they played board games all morning, sprawled out on the floor of the Talbots' family room.

The third day, they just spent the whole time talking. Jen kept Luke enthralled with stories of places she'd been, people she'd met, things she'd seen.

"When I was little, Mom used to take me to a play group that was all third children," Jen said. She giggled. "The thing was, it was all Government officials' kids. I think some of the parents didn't even like kids—they just thought it was a status symbol to break the Population Law and get away with it."

"What'd you do at the play group?" Luke asked.

"Played, of course. Everybody had a lot of toys. And one

of the kids had a dog he brought with him sometimes, and we all took turns feeding it dog biscuits."

"These people had pets, too?" Luke asked incredulously.

"Well, you know, they were Barons," Jen said.

Luke frowned. He slid down in the soft couch, so different from anything in his own house.

"My dad says that when he was little, just about everyone he knew had pets. He had a dog named Bootsy and a cat named Stripe. He talks about them all the time. Why'd the Government make pets illegal?"

"Oh, you know, the food thing," Jen said. She took a chocolate chip cookie from a pack they were sharing and waved it for emphasis. "Without dogs and cats, there's more food for humans. My dad says if it weren't for the Barons breaking the law, lots of species would have gone extinct."

Luke looked at the cookie in his own hand. So now was he supposed to feel guilty about eating food that should have gone to animals, as well as to other people?

Jen saw his expression. "Hey, don't go dopey on me," she said. "It's all a scam, remember? There's more than enough food in the world, especially now that there aren't enough babies being born."

"What?" Luke asked.

"Well, besides passing the Population Law, the Government went on this big campaign to make women think it was something evil to get pregnant and have kids. They put posters up in all the cities, with things like, 'Who's the worst criminal?' under a picture of a pregnant lady and, I don't know, some tough-looking crooks. And then if you read the whole sign it'd tell you the woman was the worst of all. Another one"—Jen giggled—"it had a picture of a huge pregnant belly, with the label, 'Ladies, do you want to look like this?' And women aren't allowed to go anywhere once they get pregnant. So now, my dad told me, there are so few babies being born that the population's going to be cut in half."

Luke shook his head, confused as usual. "So why doesn't the Government take down the signs and let people have as many babies as they want?"

Jen rolled her eyes. "Luke, you've got to quit thinking this makes any sense," Jen said. "It's the Government, remember? That's why we've got to have the rally—"

Luke changed the subject as quickly as he could. "What do women do if they can't go anywhere the whole time they're pregnant? I don't know about humans, but pigs take almost four months to have a baby. Do the women stay home all that time?"

"Hiding like us, you mean?" Jen asked. But she took the distraction. "Lots of them pretend they're just getting fat. My mom said she went shopping the day before I was born, and nobody noticed. But that's my mom and shopping."

And then she was off on a tale about her mother taking Jen shopping in a city ten hours away, just because she'd heard a store sold good purses there.

"That's probably the only reason my brothers don't turn me in," Jen said. "If she didn't have me, my mother would drag them around shopping. Can you see those two gorillas with shopping bags?"

Jen did an impression, walking around with her arms dragging from imaginary loaded-down bags. Even though Luke had only seen her brothers from a distance, he caught the resemblance and laughed.

"Your brothers would never turn you in," he protested. "Would they?"

"Of course not," Jen agreed. "They lo-ove me." She hugged herself mockingly and flopped back onto the couch beside Luke. "Anyhow, they wouldn't be smart enough to figure out how to turn me in without getting the rest of the family in trouble. What about your brothers?"

"They're not stupid," Luke said defensively. "Or—do you mean—"

"Would they ever betray you?" Jen narrowed her eyes, truly curious. "Not now, necessarily, but, say, years from now, if your parents were dead and it wouldn't hurt anybody but you, and they'd get lots of money for it—"

It was a question Luke had never considered. But he knew the answer.

"Never," he said, his voice cracking with earnestness. "I can trust them. I mean, we grew up together."

It was strange how he could be so sure, because they barely took time even to tease him anymore. Matthew was getting very serious with his girlfriend, and spent every spare moment at her house. Mark had suddenly gone basketball-crazy, and talked Dad into nailing an old tire rim to the front of the barn for a hoop. Luke could hear him outside, throwing balls late into the night. No matter how certain he was of their loyalty, Luke sometimes felt like his brothers had outgrown him. He missed them.

But it didn't matter. He had Jen now.

Luke kept Jen from talking about the rally the rest of that day, and they didn't even go near the computer. They just had fun. He crawled back to his house a few hours later, thinking that he didn't mind at all anymore, having to hide. He could go on this way forever, as long as he got to visit Jen. The leaves would come back to the trees soon, and he'd feel even safer on his trips to her house. And when planting season started, Dad would be out in the fields all day, and Luke could see Jen all the time.

But April came before planting season.

MARGARET PETERSON HADDIX

CHAPTER *TWENTY-TWO*

t rained the first two weeks of April, and Luke was in a tizzy wondering when he would ever get to see Jen again. Finally the ground dried out, and Dad headed out to the fields to plow. Luke raced to Jen's house.

"Oh, good!" she greeted him. "You can get the advance battle plans. I was afraid we were just going to have to pick you up Thursday night and fill you in then."

Luke carefully slid the door shut behind him and straightened the blinds so he and Jen would be totally hidden. Then he turned to face her.

"What are you talking about?" he asked. But he knew. His heart began to thump harder than it had in his rush through the backyards.

"The rally, of course," Jen said impatiently. "Everything's set. I'm taking one of my parents' cars, and I'm picking up three other kids on my way. But I made sure there'd be room for you. You should feel lucky—lots of kids are just going to walk. We're all meeting at the president's house at 6 A.M."

Luke clutched the cord to the blinds.

"Do you know how to drive?" he asked.

"Well enough." She flashed him a wicked grin. "My brothers told me how. Come on."

She waved him over to the couch. He sank into it while Jen perched on the edge.

"What if the Population Police stop you before you get to the capital?" he asked.

"Us, you mean. We. You're going, too, remember? Don't worry—nobody'll stop us." She giggled. "I checked the national employee staffing schedules through the computer. Let's just say several of the Population Police got some unexpected days off."

"You mean you changed their schedules? You can do that?"

Jen nodded, a wicked gleam in her eye.

"It took me a whole month to figure out how, but you are now looking at an accomplished hacker."

Dimly, Luke realized why Jen had seemed so relaxed and happy on his last several visits. They'd been vacations for her, breaks from intense work on plans for the rally. He looked closer and saw the fatigue in her eyes. She looked like a younger version of Mom after a twelve-hour shift in the chicken factory, or Dad after a long day of baling hay. But there was something more in her expression—his parents had never looked so feverishly giddy.

"What if someone finds out what you did? And changes it back?"

Jen shook her head. "They won't. I was very selective—

I coordinated everyone's travel plans and only eliminated the police who had to be eliminated. Aren't you excited? We're going to be free after all these years." She leaned down and pulled a sheaf of papers out from under the couch. "Best hiding place in the world. The maid's too lazy to clean under there. Now, let's see, I'll pick you up at 10 P.M., and—"

Luke was glad she was looking at the papers instead of him. He wouldn't have been able to meet her eyes.

"Okay, okay, so nobody's going to be caught on the way to the capital. But once you're there, at the president's house, someone will call the Population Police, and then—" Luke felt panicky just thinking about it.

Jen wasn't fazed. "So what?" she asked. "I don't care who gets called once we're there. Heck, I may call the Population Police myself. They're not going to do anything to a crowd of a thousand, especially not when lots of us are related to Government officials. We'll make them listen to us. We're a revolution!"

Luke looked away. "But your friends—you were mad at them because they weren't into it—what if they don't show up?"

"What do you mean?" Jen's voice was fierce.

Luke could barely speak for the panic welling inside him. "In the chat room, they were making jokes. Carlos and Sean and the others. You said they weren't taking it seriously."

"Oh, *that*. That was—a long time ago. They're all on

board. They're psyched. Why, Carlos is my lieutenant in all of this. You wouldn't believe how much he's helped. So, okay, ten o'clock, and then it's eight hours to the capital, and—" she consulted her papers again. "What kind of sign do you want to carry? 'I deserve a life' or 'End the Population Law now!' or—this is one I found in an old book—'Give me liberty or give me death'?"

Luke tried to imagine what Jen seemed to be taking for granted. He could get in a car. He'd sat in the pickup in the barn—a car wasn't much different. And for eight hours, that would be all he had to do—sit. Not that difficult. Except that panic would be coursing through him for the entire eight hours because of where the car was going. And then to get out, in public, at the president's house? And carry a sign? His imagination failed. He broke out in a cold sweat.

"Jen, I—" he started.

"Yes?"

Jen waited. The silence between them seemed to be growing, like a balloon. Luke struggled to speak.

"I can't go."

Jen gaped at him.

"I can't," he said again, weakly.

Jen shook her head briskly. "Yes, you can," she said. "I know you're scared—who isn't? But this is important. Do you want to hide all your life, or do you want to change history?"

Luke made a stab at humor.

"Isn't there another choice?"

Jen didn't laugh. She sprang from the couch.

"Another choice. Another choice." She paced, then jerked back to face Luke. "Sure. You can be a coward and hope someone else changes the world for you. You can hide up in that attic of yours until someone knocks at your door and says, 'Oh, yeah, they freed the hidden. Want to come out?' Is that what you want?"

Luke didn't answer.

"You've got to come, Luke, or you'll hate yourself the rest of your life. When you don't have to hide anymore, even years from now, there'll always be some small part of you whispering, 'I don't deserve this. I didn't fight for it. I'm not worth it.' And you are, Luke, you are. You're smart and funny and nice, and you should be living life, instead of being buried alive in that old house of yours—"

"Maybe I just don't mind hiding as much as you do," Luke whispered.

Jen faced him squarely, her gaze unwavering.

"Yes, you do. You hate walls as much as I do. Maybe more. Have you ever listened to yourself? Every time you talk about how you used to go outdoors and work in the garden or something, you glow. You're alive. Even if you don't want anything else, don't you want to get the outdoors back?"

What Luke wanted was to get away from Jen. Because she was right. Everything she said was right. But that couldn't mean he had to go. He huddled deeper in the couch.

"I'm not brave like you," he said.

Jen grabbed his shoulders and peered into his eyes.

"Oh, yeah?" she said. "You dared to come over here, didn't you? And here's something—why are you always the one who makes the trip? Ever think of that? If I'm so much braver, how come I'm not risking my life to see you?"

There were a thousand answers to that. *Because I found you first. Because your house is safer than mine. Because I need you more than you need me. You've got your computer and all your chat room friends. And you go places.* Luke squirmed away.

"My dad hangs around my house too much," he said. "It's safer this way. I'm—I'm just protecting you."

Jen backed up. "Thanks for the chivalry," she said bitterly. "I've got enough people protecting me. If you care so much, why don't you help me get free? You say you won't come to the rally for yourself—so do it for me. That's all I'll ever ask of you."

Luke winced. When she put things that way, how could he not go? Except—he couldn't.

"You're crazy," he said. "I can't go, and neither should you. It's too dangerous."

Jen flashed him a look of pure disgust.

"You can leave now," she said coldly. "I don't have time for you."

Luke could feel the ice in her words. He stood up.

"But—"

"Go," Jen said.

Luke stumbled toward the door. He stopped by the blinds and turned around.

"Jen, can't you understand? I do want it to work. I hope—"

"Hope doesn't mean anything," Jen snapped. "Action's the only thing that counts."

Luke backed out the door. He stood on the Talbots' patio, blinking in the sunlight, breathing in the smell of fresh air and danger. Then he turned and ran home.

CHAPTER *TWENTY-THREE*

Luke let the kitchen door slam behind him and didn't care. He was so mad, his eyes blurred. The nerve of her, saying *I don't have time for you.* Who did she think she was? He tramped up the stairs. She'd always thought she was better than him, just because she was a Baron, showing off with her soda and her potato chips and her fancy computer. So what? It didn't mean she was special, just because her parents had lots of money. It wasn't like she'd earned it or anything. Who was she, anyway? Just some dumb old girl. He wished he'd never gone over there. All she did was brag, brag, brag and show off. That's all the rally was, anyhow, showing off: *Hey, look, I'm a third child and I can go to the president's house and nobody will hurt me.* He hoped someone shot her. That would show her.

Luke stopped in the middle of pulling the attic door shut behind him. No, no, he took it back. He didn't want anyone to shoot her. His knees went weak, and he had to sit down on the stairs, all his anger suddenly turned to fear. What if someone did shoot her? He remembered the sign she'd asked if he wanted to carry: "Give me liberty or give me death." Was she serious? Did she expect to—? He stopped himself from thinking the rest. What if she never came back? He should go, if only to protect Jen. But he couldn't—

Luke buried his face in his hands, trying to hide from his own thoughts.

Mother found him there, hours later, still crouched on the stairs.

"Luke! Were you getting impatient waiting for me to get home? Did you have a nice day?"

Luke stared at her as though she were a vision from another life.

"I—" he started, ready to spill everything. He couldn't hold it all in.

Mother felt his forehead.

"Are you sick? You're so pale—I worry about you, Luke, all day long. But then I remind myself, you're safe here at home, out of harm's way." She gave him a weary smile and ruffled his hair.

Luke swallowed hard and recovered himself. What was he thinking? He couldn't tell anyone about Jen. He couldn't betray her.

"I'm fine," he lied. "I just haven't been out in the sun for a while, remember. Not that I'm complaining, of course," he added hastily.

Hiding again.

CHAPTER *TWENTY-FOUR*

For three days, Luke agonized. Sometimes he decided he had to stop Jen, to persuade her not to go. Sometimes he decided he ought to go with her. Sometimes he was mad again, and thought he should just stalk over there and demand an apology.

But anything he might do required seeing Jen, and that wasn't possible. It poured every day, the rain coming down in long, dreary sheets that made Luke feel worse as he watched from the attic vents. Downstairs he could hear Dad stomping around, muttering every now and then about the time and topsoil being lost with every raindrop. Luke felt like a prisoner.

Thursday night he went to bed convinced he'd never be able to sleep for imagining Jen and the others in her car, getting farther and farther from him and closer and closer to danger. But he must have dozed off, because he woke to total darkness. His heart pounded. He was sweaty. Had he dreamed something? Had he heard something? A floorboard creaked. His ears roared as he tried to listen. Was that someone else's breath or just his own, loud and scared? A beam of light swept across his face.

"Luke?" A whisper.

Luke bolted up in bed.

"Jen? Is that you?"

She switched off her flashlight.

"Yes. I thought I'd kill myself coming up your stairs. Why didn't you tell me they were so narrow?" She sounded like the same old Jen, not mad. Not crazy.

"I didn't know you'd ever be climbing them," Luke said.

It was insane to be talking about stairs now, in the middle of the night, in his room. Every word either of them spoke was dangerous. Mother was a light sleeper. But Luke was delighted not to be moving on, not to be talking about what Jen had really come to talk about.

"Your parents didn't lock your doors," Jen said. She seemed to be stalling, too. "Guess I'm lucky the Government outlawed pets. Didn't farmers always used to keep big guard dogs that would chomp people's heads off in one bite?"

Luke shrugged, then remembered Jen couldn't see him in the dark. "Jen, I—" He wasn't sure what he was going to say until he said it. "I still can't go. I'm sorry. It's something about having parents who are farmers, not lawyers. And not being a Baron. It's people like you who change history. People like me—we just let things happen to us."

"No. You're wrong. You can make things happen—"

Luke sensed, rather than saw, Jen shaking her head. Even in the dark, he could visualize each precisely cut strand of hair bouncing and falling back into place.

"I'm sorry," she continued. "I didn't come here to harp at you. This is dangerous, and no one should go unwillingly. I was too hard on you the other day. I just wanted to say—you've been a good friend. I'll miss you."

"But you'll be back," Luke said. "Tomorrow—or the next day—after the rally. I'll be over to visit. If your rally works, I'll be walking in the front door."

"We can hope," Jen said softly. Her voice faded away. "Good-bye, Luke."

CHAPTER *TWENTY-FIVE*

Luke lay awake the rest of the night. At first light, he got up and quietly scrubbed away the mud Jen had tracked in and up the stairs. Trust her not to think about mud. He fervently hoped she'd thought of all the details about the rally.

Luke was just finishing the last of the kitchen floor when he heard the toilet flushing upstairs. He hid the muddy rags in the trash and scrambled back to his place on the stairs just in time to meet Mother coming down.

"'Morning, early bird." She yawned. "Were you up during the night? I thought I heard something."

"I had trouble sleeping," Luke said truthfully.

Mother yawned again.

"And you're up early...feeling okay?"

"Just hungry," Luke said.

But he picked at his food. Everything he ate stuck in his throat.

After the rest of his family left, he risked sneaking over and turning the radio on low. There were weather reports and commercials for soybean seed and lots of music.

"Come on, come on," he muttered, keeping one eye on the side window, watching for Dad.

Finally the radio voice announced the news. Someone's cattle had gotten out and caused a minor car wreck. Nobody hurt. A Government spokesman predicted a poor planting season because of all the rain.

Nothing about the rally.

Dad came back toward the house. Luke snapped off the radio and bolted for the stairs.

At lunch, Dad forgot to turn the radio on, and Luke had to remind him. The announcer promised a big story after the commercials. His sandwich gone, Dad reached over to turn the radio off.

"No, no—wait!" Luke said. "This might be interesting—"

Dad harrumphed, but waited.

The announcer came back. He cleared his throat and declared that new Government statistics proved last year's alfalfa harvest had set a record for the decade.

It was like that for days. Luke kept waiting, desperate to hear anything. But the few times he could get to the radio, it said nothing.

Every time Dad left the house for any length of time, Luke switched on the light by the back door, his old signal to Jen. He stared so hard, willing her answering light to go on, that he thought he would go blind. But there was nothing.

He took to watching her house as obsessively as he had when he had first discovered her existence. There was no sign of her. The rest of her family came and went as usual. Did they look sadder? Happy? Worried? At peace? From a distance, he couldn't tell.

He got so desperate, he asked Mother if she'd thought about going over to visit the new neighbors, to welcome them to the area. She looked at him as if he were deranged.

"They've been there for months. They're hardly new anymore. And they're *Barons*," she said. She laughed in a way that didn't hide her bitterness. "Believe me, they don't want us visiting."

And what was she supposed to do, say, "Nice to meet you. Now, tell me everything about the child you never talk about"?

After a week, Luke did feel deranged. Every time anyone spoke to him, he jumped. Mother asked him, "Are you all right?" so many times, he took to avoiding her. But he couldn't just sit in the attic, waiting. He paced. He fidgeted. He chewed his fingernails.

He came up with a plan.

CHAPTER *TWENTY-SIX*

Finally, finally, a week and a half after the rally, a day dawned that was so clear and dry, Luke knew Dad would be in the fields all day. Without hope, Luke turned on the light by the back door. After five minutes without a response, he turned it off and quietly slipped out the door.

The cool air was a jolt, and for the briefest time, he paused. This was more dangerous than ever.

"But I have to *know*," he muttered fiercely, and crept alongside the barn before making his dash for Jen's house.

He had to rip the screen and break the pane of one of the Talbot's windows, which he felt bad about. But it didn't matter. If Jen was there, she could think of an excuse. And if she wasn't…if she wasn't, he'd never be back at the Talbots' again.

Once inside, he knew he had to do something about the alarm quickly. Jen had explained it to him once, told him the exact sequence of buttons to hit to disable it. He ran to the hall closet, yanked open the door, and punched buttons quickly, afraid he'd forget the sequence if he hesitated even a second. Green-blue-yellow-green-blue-orange-red.

The lights blinked out before he hit the last button, and that spooked him. Was that how it worked before?

"Hurry, hurry," he urged himself. The words kept replaying in his brain.

"Jen?" he called. "Jen?"

He went up and down stairs, looking in every room.

"Jen? You don't have to hide. It's me. Luke."

The house was enormous, three floors and a basement. He couldn't search everywhere, but if Jen was there, why would she hide? Against reason, he kept hoping she was.

"Jen? Come on. This isn't funny."

He found the bedrooms—huge, elegant rooms with beautifully carved beds and long, mirrored closets. He couldn't even tell which one was Jen's.

Finally, he admitted defeat and rushed down to the computer room.

He hurried over to the keyboard and typed in the same sequence of letters he'd watched Jen type so many times. His fingers were clumsy, and he kept messing up. Finally, he got to the chat room password. F-E-R-E. No. Erase. F-E-E-R. No. At last he got it. F-R-E-E.

The screen went blank, with none of the friendly banter that had magically appeared every time he'd watched Jen. Had he done something wrong? Frantically, he exited and entered the chat room again, his hands shaking. Still nothing. Timidly, using only his right index finger, he typed, "Where's Jen?" He had to hold one hand with the other to steady his finger enough to hit the Enter button.

Almost instantaneously, his words vanished and reappeared at the top of the screen. He waited. Nothing. The screen stayed blank below his question.

Because nothing was worse than doing nothing, he typed again, "Hello? Is anybody there?"

Still nothing. He slammed his fist down on the computer desk so hard, it hurt.

"I have to know!" he shouted. "Tell me! I can't go home until I know!"

He heard the door too late to react. And suddenly a voice boomed behind him: "Turn around slowly. I have a gun. Who are you and why are you here?"

CHAPTER *TWENTY-SEVEN*

Luke stifled his instinct to run. He turned around as slowly as he could. Guns had been outlawed for everyone but Government officials long before he was born. But he recognized the object pointed at him from books and Dad's descriptions. Dad had always talked about hunting rifles and shotguns, big guns to bring down deer or wolves. This gun was smaller. Meant to kill humans.

All that flashed through Luke's mind before he looked beyond the gun, to the man holding it. He was tall and fleshy, his expensive clothes only partially hiding his bulk. Luke had seen him only from a distance before.

"You're Jen's dad," he said.

"I didn't ask who I was," the man snapped. "Who are you?"

Luke exhaled slowly.

"A friend of Jen's," he said cautiously.

Only because he was watching very, very closely did he see the man lower the gun by a fraction of an inch.

"Please," Luke said. "I just want to know where she is."

This time the man clearly relaxed his gun hand. He circled around behind Luke and snapped off the computer.

"Jen says you have to park the hard drive before you do that," Luke said.

"How do you know about Jen?" the man asked. He narrowed his eyes.

Luke blinked. The man was bargaining, he realized, offering to negotiate. He wanted something from Luke before he would tell Luke anything about Jen. But what?

"I'm a third child, too," Luke said finally. The man's expression didn't change, but Luke thought he saw a flicker of interest in his eyes. "I'm a neighbor. I found out about her, and I started coming over, when I could."

"How did you know she was here?" the man said.

"I saw—" Luke didn't want to get her in trouble. "I saw lights when I knew everyone was gone. I guessed. I—I really wanted there to be another third child for me to meet."

"So Jen was careless," the man said, with an edge to his voice that Luke didn't understand.

"No," Luke said uncertainly. "I was observant."

The man nodded, only to accept Luke's answer. Then he sat down in the chair by the computer desk, and rested the gun on his leg. Luke took that as a sign that the conversation might last long enough for him to find out something.

"Did Jen teach you how to disable our alarm system?" the man asked.

Luke saw no point in lying. "Yes. But I must have screwed up, since you came—"

"No," the man said. "If you'd screwed up, the security

guards would have come. But I have it set so I'm automatically notified if the system's shut down while I'm away.... Given the circumstances, I decided to investigate myself."

Luke longed to ask what "circumstances" he meant, but the man was already asking another question. "So what else did you and Jen do together?" the man said. Luke couldn't understand why he sounded so accusatory.

"Nothing," Luke said. "I mean, we talked a lot. She showed me the computer. She—she wanted me to go to the rally, but I was too scared."

Too late, Luke thought to wonder if the man knew about the rally. Was Luke betraying Jen's confidence? But the man didn't seem surprised. He was studying Luke as intently as Luke had been studying him.

"Why didn't you stop her?" the man asked.

"Stop Jen? That's like trying to stop the sun," Luke said.

The man gave Luke the faintest of smiles, one that contained no happiness. "Just remember that," he said.

"So where is she?" Luke asked.

The man looked away.

"Jen's—" His voice broke. "Jen is no longer with us."

"She—?"

"She's dead," the man said harshly.

Somehow Luke had known without wanting to know. He still stumbled backwards, in shock. He bumped into the couch and sagged into it.

"No," he said. "Not Jen. No. You're lying."

His ears roared. He thought crazy things. *This is a dream.*

A nightmare. I will make myself wake up. He remembered Jen talking a mile a minute, gesturing wildly. How could she be dead? He tried to picture her lying still, not moving. Dead. It was impossible.

The man was shaking his head helplessly.

"I'd give anything to have her back," he whispered. "But it's true. I saw. They gave us...they gave us the body. Special privilege for a Government official." His voice was so bitter, Luke could barely listen. "And we couldn't even bury her in the family plot. Couldn't take a bereavement day off work. Couldn't tell anyone why we're going around with red eyes and aching hearts. No—we just had to pretend to be the same old family of four we'd always been."

"How?" Luke asked. "How did she...die?"

He was thinking, if the car had wrecked, it wouldn't be so bad. Or maybe it had nothing to do with the rally. Maybe she just got really sick.

"They shot her," Jen's father said. "They shot all of them. All forty kids at the rally, gunned down right in front of the president's house. The blood flowed into his rose-bushes. But they had the sidewalks scrubbed before the tourists came, so nobody would know."

Luke started shaking his head no, and couldn't stop.

"But Jen said there'd be too many people to shoot. She said there'd be a thousand," Luke protested, as if Jen's words could change what he was hearing.

"Our Jen had too much faith in the bravery of her fellow hidden," Jen's father said.

Luke flinched. "I told her I couldn't go," he said. "I told her! It's not my fault!"

"No," Jen's dad said quietly. "And you couldn't have stopped her. It's not your fault. There are plenty of other people who deserve the blame. They probably would have shot a thousand. Or fifteen thousand. They don't care."

His face twisted. Luke thought he had never seen such pain, not even the time Matthew dropped a sledgehammer on his foot. Tears began to spill down Jen's father's face.

"What I don't understand is—why did she do this, this Children's Crusade? She wasn't stupid. We'd been warning her about the Population Police all her life. Did she really think the rally would work?" he said.

"Yes," Luke assured him. Then, unbidden, the last words she'd spoken to him came back to him: *We can hope*—after she'd told him hope was worthless. Maybe she knew the rally would fail. Maybe she even knew she would probably die. He remembered the first day he'd met her, when she'd cut her hand to cover the drops of his blood on the carpet. There was something strange in Jen he couldn't quite understand, that made her willing to sacrifice herself to help others. Or to try to.

"I think at first she thought the rally would work," Luke told Jen's dad. "And then, even when she wasn't sure...she still had to go. She wouldn't call it off."

"Why?" Jen's dad asked. He was sobbing. "Did she want to die?"

"No," Luke said. "She wanted to live. Not die. Not hide. Live."

The words played over and over again in his brain: "Not hide. Live. Not hide. Live." As long as he held on to them, he felt like Jen was there. She'd just left the room for a minute, to get more potato chips, maybe, and soon she'd be back to lecture him again about how they both deserved a better life than hiding. He could believe it was her voice echoing in his ears.

But if he let go, let the words stop for a minute, he was lost. He felt like the whole world was spinning away from him, and he was all alone. He wanted to cry out, "Jen! Come back!"—as if she could hear him, and stop the spinning, and come to him.

As if from a great distance, Luke heard Jen's father heave a sigh and blow his nose in a businesslike way.

"You may not be ready to hear this," he said. "But—"

Dizzily, Luke raised his head and listened halfheartedly.

"When you logged into that chat room," Jen's father said, "a buzzer went off in a room in Population Police headquarters. They're monitoring the chat room very closely—they found it after the rally. I've managed to…uh, cover up things about Jen, but they'll trace your message back to our computer. The Population Police are backlogged right now, following leads from the rally, so I should have a day or two to come up with a plausible-sounding explanation. But if they investigate too carefully, you may be in danger."

"More than usual?" Luke said sarcastically.

Jen's dad took the question seriously.

"Yes. They will begin actively looking for you. They'll search every house around this one. It wouldn't take them long to find you."

A chill ran down Luke's spine. So he would die, just like Jen. Or not like her—she had gone bravely. He would be caught like a mouse in its hole.

"But if you'll let me," Jen's dad continued, "I can get you a fake I.D. You can be miles away before they come looking."

"You would do that for me?" Luke asked. "Why?"

"Because of Jen."

"But—how?"

"I have connections. You see"—Jen's dad hesitated—"I work for the Population Police."

CHAPTER TWENTY-EIGHT

Luke began screaming and couldn't stop. Suddenly his brain didn't seem to have any control whatsoever over what his body did. He felt his legs spring up and propel him toward Jen's dad. He saw his own hand grab for the gun and wrestle it away. He heard a voice he barely recognized as his own scream, again and again, "No! No! No!"

"Stop!" Jen's dad yelled. "Stop, you little fool, before you get us both killed—"

Somehow, the gun was in Luke's hand. Jen's dad lunged at him, and Luke could picture Jen's dad tackling him, just as Jen had tackled him all those months ago. But this time Luke stepped to the side at the last moment, and Jen's dad crashed uselessly into the far wall. Luke pointed the gun at him and struggled to hold it steady.

Jen's dad turned around slowly.

"You can shoot me," he said, holding his hands helplessly up in the air. "I might even welcome the chance to stop missing Jen. But it would be a mistake. I swear to you, in the name of everything that's sacred—in Jen's name— I'm on your side."

Jen's dad stared into Luke's eyes, waiting. Luke felt a surge of pride that he'd gotten the upper hand, that he had earned the right to decide what happened next. But how could he know what was right? Surely Jen's own father wouldn't lie in her name. Would he?

Luke squeezed his eyes shut. Then he lowered the gun to his side.

"Good," Jen's dad said, audibly releasing his breath.

Luke let Jen's dad walk toward him, gently take the gun, and lay it on the desk.

"I was going to explain," Jen's dad said, panting a little. He sat down. "I only work at Population Police headquarters. I don't agree with what they do. I try to sabotage them as much as I can. Jen never understood, either— sometimes you have to work from inside enemy lines."

Jen's dad talked and talked and talked. Luke thought he was repeating everything he said two or three times, but that was okay, because Luke's brain was functioning so slowly, he needed the extra help.

"Do you know much history?" Jen's dad asked.

Luke tried to remember if there were any history books among his family's collection in the attic. Did adventure stories of long ago count?

"Just—" He cleared his throat. "Just from the books Jen loaned me."

"Which ones?"

Luke pointed to the ones on the shelves above the computer.

"And she gave me some articles, printouts from the computer."

Jen's dad nodded. "So you got the propaganda from both sides," he said. "No truth."

"What do you mean?" Luke asked.

"The Government publications are trying to convince people of one thing, so they stretch the facts. And the underground is just as extreme in its own way, making statistics match their cause. So you know nothing."

"Jen said the stuff from the computer was true," Luke said defensively. Just saying her name made him wince. And now she was dead. How could she be dead?

Jen's dad waved that away impatiently.

"She believed what she wanted to. But I'm afraid—" He stopped, and Luke was afraid Jen's dad might start crying again. Then he swallowed hard and went on. "I'm afraid I encouraged her. I passed along some slanted information. I wanted to give her hope that someday the Population Law would be repealed. I didn't know she'd...she'd..."

Luke knew he wouldn't be able to bear seeing Jen's dad break down again.

"So what should I know?" Luke asked. "What is the truth?"

"The truth," Jen's dad muttered, catching onto those two words as though Luke had thrown him a lifeline. He recovered himself quickly. "Nobody really knows. There have been too many lies for too long. Our Government is totalitarian, and totalitarian governments never like truth."

That made no sense to Luke, but he let Jen's dad go on talking.

"You know about the famines?"

Luke nodded.

"Before that, our country believed in freedom and democracy and equality for all. Then the famines came, and the government was overthrown. There were riots in every city, over food, and many, many people were killed. When General Sherwood came to power, he promised law and order and food for all. By then, that was all the people wanted. And all they got."

Luke squinted, trying to understand. This was grown-up talk, pure and simple. No, it was worse than the grown-up talk he was used to, because all his parents ever talked about was the corn harvest and bills and the likelihood of frost at the end of May. Those Luke understood. Governments being overthrown, cities rioting—they were beyond his comprehension.

"Barons got more," he blurted, then blushed because it sounded so rude.

Jen's dad laughed. "True. You noticed. I know it's not fair, and I'm not proud of it, but...Government officials made a conscious decision to allow one class of people to have special privileges—Jen probably introduced you to junk food, didn't she?"

Luke nodded.

"That's a good example. Officially, it's illegal, but no one ever got arrested for supplying Barons with junk food. Which is mighty convenient, considering that all the powerful Government officials are Barons." The cynicism in his voice sounded so much like Jen that Luke almost gave in to grief again. But he forced himself to focus on what Jen's dad was saying.

"The Government justifies keeping everyone else in poverty because people seem to work the hardest when they're right on the edge of survival," he continued. "The Government does try to make sure that most people—the ones who cooperate—do survive. If you've heard your parents talking about other farmers, you'll know that nobody loses their farms anymore. But, also, nobody ever makes enough to live comfortably."

Luke thought about his parents' constant worries about money. Was it all unnecessary? Were they just being manipulated? He felt a spark of anger, but buried that, too, because he had other questions.

"But even Barons have to follow the Population Law," he said. "Is that because"—he gulped—"because it's necessary? Were there too many people? Are there?"

"Probably not," Jen's dad said. "If food had been distributed fairly…if people hadn't panicked…if we'd had good leaders being honest about the need for everyone's cooperation…we could have survived the crisis without curtailing anyone's rights. And now—it shouldn't be a problem if some people choose to have three or four kids, as long as some other people choose to have none. But the Population Law became General Sherwood's proudest accomplishment. That's why even Barons aren't exempt. He points to that and says, 'See how much control I have over my people's lives.'"

"So it is wrong," Luke said, trying to grasp the point.

"I believe so. Yes," Jen's dad said.

Luke felt a strange sense of relief, that it wasn't truly wrong for him to exist, just illegal. For the first time since he'd read the Government books, he could see the two things being separate. Maybe that was why he'd been too scared to go to the rally. If he'd truly believed, the way Jen had, then he might have gone.

And would he have been killed, as she was?

It was all too confusing and scary to think about.

Jen's father looked at his watch.

"I need to get back to work. I can only hide so much. If you want it, I can have the fake I.D. for you by tomorrow night. In the meantime, I'd advise you to—"

He broke off. Luke knew why: a sound from his worst nightmares—pounding on the door, and then the command, "Open up! Population Police!"

CHAPTER TWENTY-NINE

Before Luke had a chance to move, Jen's dad had picked him up and thrust him into the closet.

"There's a secret door at the back," he hissed. "Use it."

Luke groped blindly, fighting through what felt like piles of hair. Behind him, he could hear Jen's dad yelling, "I'm coming! I'm coming! That's a twelve-thousand-dollar door. If you break it down, you're going to pay!" Then Luke heard the computer making its *be-be-be-beeep!* and Jen's dad muttering, "Fine time for them to discover efficiency. Come on, come on, connect—"

The pounding at the door grew louder, and a gruff voice yelled out, "You have three seconds, George!"

Luke dug deeper into the closet. He couldn't even find the back wall, let alone any secret door. And then he heard a splintering sound from the front of the house. Seconds later, there were stomping footsteps in the computer room.

"What is the meaning of this?"

It was Jen's dad's voice coming from the hall, full of outrage. If he hadn't witnessed it himself, Luke never would have guessed that Jen's dad had been crying only moments before. He sounded too forceful, too assured, too confident that he was right and anyone who opposed him was wrong. The stomping stopped. From deep inside the closet, Luke heard someone snicker.

"Caught you with your pants down, eh, George?"

"Yes, yes, very funny," Jen's father replied, not sounding the least bit amused. There was a sound that could have been a zipper being zipped. "Has it come to this? A man can't even go to the bathroom without his door being broken down by a bunch of morons with power complexes? And you will pay for that door, I assure you."

If Luke had been one of the Population Police, Jen's dad would have scared him to pieces. Luke would have backed out, muttering, "I'm sorry. I'm sorry." He never would have believed that Jen's dad was hiding a third child. Hopefully, Luke paused in his burrowing into the Talbots' closet.

But the voice that answered Jen's father carried only the slightest edge of doubt.

"Come off it, George. You know we're entitled to search and seizure. We have reports of that computer being used for illegal purposes. Just a half an hour ago."

"You're even bigger fools than I thought," Jen's dad answered. "Don't any of you read your memos? I reported to Central Command this morning that I was going to continue my sting operation in the illegal chat rooms. See, I wrote, 'Where's Jen?' and, 'Hello? Is anybody there?', which is what some lost, confused, third child who missed the rally might write. Are you so low-ranking that you don't know I was pretending to be the guerrilla leader Jen all along? Did you miss the commendation ceremony where I was rewarded for the disposal of forty illegals?"

Luke wondered that Jen's dad could say her name without his voice giving him away. If Luke didn't know Jen—hadn't known her, he corrected himself with a wince—and if he didn't know how much she'd trusted her father, he would have been certain that Jen's father had double-crossed her. As it was, his head swam with the fear that Jen's father still might betray him. How could he trust anyone who spoke so coldly of the "disposal" of third children? Luke struggled on through the closet, reaching a stack of blankets at the back. Finally he touched the wall, but everything he felt was smooth. Jen's father said there was a door. There had to be a door.

The voices from outside the closet were muffled now.

"—see the memo—"

"I'm sure it's on your desk back at the office, with all the paperwork you never read." Jen's dad raised his voice, so Luke could hear him clearly. "Or can you even read?"

The Population Police officer ignored the insult.

"Show us on the computer."

"Very well."

Luke prayed that Jen's dad had something to show them. He could not find the door, though he ran his fingers along the wall, again and again. His heart was beating so loudly, he was sure the Population Police could hear him.

All he could hear of the Population Police and Jen's father were mutterings. Then the one officer's voice rang out, "You're lying, George. We're going to search."

"Just because of a computer malfunction? Fine. It's not my problem." Luke was stunned by the indifference in Jen's father's voice. "But when you don't find anything—and you won't—you know that I'm entitled to the Illegal Search and Seizure Benefits granted to Barons, and I will press charges. Should I use the extra money on caviar or champagne?"

"Aw, George, you wouldn't really sue."

"You don't think so? Then go ahead. Start here."

Suddenly the closet was flooded with light. Luke stifled a gasp. How could Jen's father have flung open the door of the very place Luke was hiding? Desperately, Luke yanked a blanket over his head.

None of the Population Police answered Jen's father, but the pattern of shadows that fell on Luke's blanket made him think the Population Police were standing right in the doorway of the closet. He heard hangers scraping against a metal bar. And then the Population Police walked away.

Confused and terrified, Luke remained huddled under the blanket. He could hear muffled footfalls elsewhere in the house, and was certain they'd be returning to the computer room any minute. Before they killed him, he hoped they let him go back to his parents and tell them how much he loved them. He could apologize to Matthew and Mark, too, for not appreciating the checkers and card games they played with him when he knew they'd rather be outside. And probably he should apologize to his parents for disobeying, and coming to Jen's house in the first place. Except, even scared to death of being found, he couldn't scrape up full regret for that.

Anyhow, it wasn't likely that they'd let him see his parents before they killed him. He'd have to protect his parents, and refuse to even reveal who they were....

Luke's mind was still racing with frantic plans when he heard someone coming back to the computer room. There was only one set of footsteps, so he dared to hope—

"You could have swept up the glass on your way out!"

It was Jen's dad. Luke strained to hear an answer, but none came. Were the Population Police gone?

Luke kept his head down. He heard Jen's dad wading into the closet. Then he pulled the blanket off Luke and clamped his hand over Luke's mouth. Luke started to struggle until he read the words on the paper Jen's dad held in front of his face:

They're gone.

You're safe,

but

DON'T TALK!!!

Luke relaxed and nodded to show he would obey. Jen's dad released him, flipped the paper over, and began writing furiously.

House bugged now.

Luke gave Jen's dad a puzzled look.

"B—" he started to say, then remembered and stopped. He took the pen from Jen's dad and wrote, *Bugged? Ants? Roaches?*

Jen's dad shook his head frantically. *Bugs = little listening devices—Population Police hear everything. That's why can't talk. They do that when a bust's unsuccessful. Even left one bug on me.*

Jen's dad turned around and pointed, and Luke saw a small disc sticking to the back of his collar.

Luke frowned and wrote on the paper, *Why not take off?*

Jen's dad shook his head. *Safer this way. Long as they think they hear everything, they won't come back.*

Jen's dad pointed to the hairy lumps on the hangers behind him.

Bribed them with fur coats. Very rare, very valuable.

Luke looked at the coats. There did seem to be a lot fewer of them now. Were they animal skins? Why would anyone want such a thing? He couldn't ask, though, because Jen's dad was already scribbling more.

Just bought time. My goose probably cooked now—I didn't file that memo. They'll find out.

Luke reached for the pen. *What will they do to you?*

Jen's dad shook his head. *Don't know,* he wrote. *I've survived this kind of thing before. But everything's chancy now. The fact they got here so fast = they have it in for me.*

Weakly, Luke leaned his head back against the closet wall. That reminded him of his frantic search along its surface. He reached for the paper and wrote, *Where's the door?*

Jen's dad pulled out a new sheet of paper. Shaking his head, he wrote, *Isn't one. Just wanted to get you to back of closet.*

Luke buried his face in his hands. Jen's dad was a good liar, there was no doubt about that. How could Luke trust him? Luke raised his head and watched as Jen's dad scribbled something else on the paper. His expression was full of concern, and Luke knew, somehow, that he was trustworthy. He easily could have turned Luke in, and gotten praise and another commendation ceremony. But how confusing, to never know when someone was lying.

Jen's dad turned the paper to face Luke. It said, *So. Want fake I.D. or not?*

Luke gulped. After a minute, he wrote back, *Am I safe if I don't?*

Jen's dad seemed to be weighing the question. He narrowed his eyes and wrote, *Probably. They're after me now, not you. If they really thought there was an illegal here, they wouldn't take bribe. Or would take it and you, too. But I'd advise—get I.D.*

Luke wrote back, *Can't I wait? Think about it for a while?*

That was what Luke wanted. Or not even to think, but to hide from thinking for a while. He wanted to remember Jen, and grieve for her by himself. He didn't want to have to think about what parts of the Population Law were good, and what parts were bad, or why his family didn't have more money. He didn't want to have to figure out Jen's dad, and other people like him, who could pretend to be so many different things. He didn't want to have to decide something now that could change the rest of his life.

But Jen's dad had written back, *Don't know. May be case of 'now or never.'*

Luke scrawled, *Why?*

Jen's dad wrote for a long time. Then he turned the paper to Luke. It said: *I have power now. Tomorrow, probably. Next week????? Next year????? Can't tell with our Gov't. Favored lackey one day,* persona non grata *the next. Never know. No guarantees.*

Luke stared at the paper until the words blurred together. He had to decide. Now.

He thought about reading and daydreaming in the attic the rest of his life. His parents were kind to him, even if they weren't around much. And as much as Matthew and Mark had always teased him, he was pretty sure they would take care of him if his parents couldn't someday. His life was very limited—he understood that now more than ever. But he was used to it. It was safe. He could make himself be happy.

Except...

Luke remembered how bored he'd felt before meeting Jen, how desperate he'd been to do something—anything!—besides read and daydream. He'd been so desperate that he'd risked his life for the chance of meeting another third child. Did he want to spend the rest of his life feeling that desperate? Did he want to just...waste it?

But even if he got a fake I.D., what would he do?

The answer was there instantly, as if he'd known it all

along and his brain was just waiting for him to come looking.

He could do something to help other third children come out of hiding. Not with another big dramatic rally, like Jen had tried, or by finding fake I.D.'s the way Jen's dad did. Maybe there was something smaller and slower he could do. Studying ways to grow more food, so no one would go hungry, no matter how many kids people had. Or changing the Government so that farmers were allowed to raise pigs or use hydroponics, and ordinary people, not just Barons, could have better lives. Or figuring out ways for people to live in outer space, so they wouldn't be too crowded on Earth and chop down beautiful woods just for houses. He didn't know exactly how he could do those things, or even what the right thing to do was. But he wanted to do something.

He remembered what he'd told Jen, the last time he'd seen her: *It's people like you who change history. People like me— we just let things happen to us.* And he'd believed it. That was how his family had always lived. But maybe that was wrong. Maybe he could succeed where Jen had failed precisely because he wasn't a Baron—because he didn't have her sense that the world owed him everything. He could be more patient, more cautious, more practical.

But he'd never be able to do anything staying in hiding.

He bit his lip. His hand shook as he wrote his answer.

I want a fake I.D. Please.

CHAPTER *THIRTY*

Lee Grant settled into the car that would take him away from the farm where he'd found refuge, after running away from home. He'd gotten lost—he'd certainly never intended to end up *here*. He surveyed the dusty barnyard in front of him, the ugly ruts of dried mud where tractors and trucks had left their tracks. He stared at the ramshackle barn and the peeling paint on the weathered house, sights that should have been entirely foreign to him, but weren't. He—

Luke gulped, unable to keep thinking in his new iden-tity quite yet. It was too soon, too hard, when his shoulders still felt the warmth of Mother's last hug. He looked down at his hands, clenched together in his lap, and they already seemed like someone else's against the background of his crisp new trousers. No more ragged blue jeans and hand-me-down flannel shirts for him—he had a whole suitcase in the trunk full of the same kind of fancy Baron clothes he'd laughed at all those months ago. He didn't care about the clothes, but he wished they'd let him keep his name, at least. Yet Jen's father had been proud that he'd gotten to keep the same initials.

"A rush job like this, it's a wonder you're not stuck with Alphonse Xerxes," he'd bragged in the letter he'd dropped off the night before, pretending he was just coming to ask Luke's parents to cut back the willow tree that draped over onto the Talbots' land.

The real Lee Grant was a Baron. He had died in a skiing accident just the night before. His parents wanted nothing to do with Luke—"too painful," Jen's father had explained— but they had agreed to donate their son's name and identity card the way people had once donated hearts and kidneys. Some secret group that helped third children had arranged it. The group also had agreed to pay for Luke to go to a private school as a boarder, year-round. Supposedly he was transferring in during the middle of a term as punishment for running away. He'd read about such places in the old books in the attic. It seemed a strange way to live, without family, but he was just as glad not to have to pretend to love another set of parents.

Now Luke looked back at his family's porch, where Mother and Dad and Matthew and Mark were standing and already waving. Dad and Matthew looked gruff, and Mark merely looked serious—strange enough for him— but tears were streaming down Mother's face.

She'd cried, too, the night Luke had told his parents everything.

He'd started with his first visit to Jen's house, and Mother had immediately scolded, "Oh, Luke, how could you? The danger…I know you're lonely, but honey, promise us, never again…"

"That's not all," Luke said.

He told the rest of the story without looking at her, until he reached the end and his decision to get a fake I.D. Then the sound of her sobbing made it impossible to avoid looking. She was red-eyed, devastated.

"Luke, no. You can't," she'd gasped. "Don't you know how we'd miss you?"

"But, Mother, I don't want to go," Luke said. "It's just that…I have to. I can't spend the rest of my life hiding in the attic. What will happen when you and Dad can't take care of me anymore?"

"Matthew or Mark will," she replied.

"But I don't want to be a burden on them. I want to do something with my life. Figure out ways to help other third kids. Make—" All the things he'd thought of sounded too childish to explain, in the face of Mother's sobbing. So he finished weakly, "Make a difference in the world."

"I'm not saying you can never do that," she answered. "But that's years away. We'll figure out some way to get a fake I.D. for you when you're grown up. Somehow." She turned to Luke's father. "Tell him, Harlan."

Dad sighed heavily.

"The boy's right. He needs to go now, if he can."

Luke could tell his father's words came out painfully, but they still stabbed at him. Maybe part of him had been secretly hoping his parents would forbid him to go, would lock him in the attic and keep him as their little boy forever.

"I've checked around some, quietlike, to see if anyone's heard of a third child getting to live a normal life. Around here, they can't," Dad said. "Far as I can tell, he's not going to get another chance."

Luke turned back to his mother, because it was too hard to look at Dad while he was saying that. But the pain twisting Mother's face was worse.

"Then I guess we don't have a choice," she'd murmured.

That had been two days ago, and ever since then she'd called in sick to work and stayed home, spending every second with Luke. They'd played board games and cards, but she'd interrupted every move with, "Do you remember..." or, "I remember..."

The coos he'd made as a baby. His first steps. His delight in discovering dirt the spring he was two. The first time he'd hoed a straight row. The zucchini he'd grown as long as his arm. The bedtime stories and tucking-ins.

She was filling him up with memories, he knew, for the times when he'd have no one to talk to about his childhood. But it was hard to listen to. He wished they could just move their Monopoly pieces and pretend the time wasn't ticking away.

But all too soon this morning had come. Jen's dad had pulled up in his fancy car, and sprang out to shake hands with Luke's parents.

"Mr. Garner, Mrs. Garner, thank you very much for reporting this boy's arrival immediately. From what I hear, the Grants were worried sick." He turned to Luke. "Young man, what you did was irresponsible and reckless. The only smart thing you did was remember to take your I.D. card. I guess you must have heard that the Population Police shoot first and ask questions later."

He clapped Luke on the back and slid his hand down to slip something into Luke's pocket. Luke reached down to touch the stiff edge of an I.D. card. His I.D. card.

"Do we have to start pretending already?" Luke's mother whispered, the tears beginning in her eyes.

Jen's dad was shaking his head sternly and patting his chest, as if looking for something in a hidden pocket.

"Bugged," he mouthed.

When Luke's parents nodded to show they understood, he stopped patting and pulled out an official-looking paper.

"Ah, here they are. Your travel papers. Your parents are sending you to Hendricks School for Boys. And if you don't shape up—" Jen's dad gave him a stern look that somehow also conveyed his sympathy.

"Would"—Mother cleared her throat—"Would it be all right if we gave him a good-bye hug? We've gotten kind of fond of him in...in the time he's been here."

Jen's father nodded, and then both Luke's parents held him tight and released him.

"Be a good boy, now, you hear?" Mother said. Luke could tell she was trying to make it jokey, the way she might talk to some other mother's runaway son. But for the life of him, he couldn't come back with a joking response. He only nodded, blinking hard.

And then he stumbled to the car and tried to be Lee.

Jen's dad circled the car and slid in on the driver's side. He started the car and pulled out.

"You're just lucky you're getting such a highly paid chauffeur," he said. "If I weren't a personal friend of your father's cousin—"

Luke wasn't sure if there was a hidden message in the words, or if Jen's dad was just talking for the sake of the bug. He decided he couldn't analyze it yet. He peered back at his frantically waving family until they were out of sight. Soon the car was passing the other side of the barn and the field beyond, views Luke had never seen, though he'd lived his entire life within a hundred yards of them. In spite of the fear gnawing in his stomach and the anguish of missing his family—already—he felt a thrill of excitement. There was so much to see. He'd have to tell Jen—

Jen. The grief he'd been avoiding for days welled over him again. But, "I'm doing this for you, too, Jen," he whispered, too softly for Jen's dad or the bug to hear over the car's hum. "Someday when we're all free, all the third children, I'll tell everyone about you. They'll erect statues to you, and name holidays after you...." It wasn't much, but it made him feel better. A little.

Luke stared back at his family's farm as long as he could. He could see just the roof of Jen's house beyond the sparse line of trees. And then, in no time at all, it seemed, everything familiar disappeared over the horizon.

Lee Grant turned around to see what lay ahead.